Lucky Brilliant

Maureen Sherbondy

Black Rose Writing | Texas

ISBN: 978-1-68433-545-9
PUBLISHED BY BLACK ROSE WRITING
www.blackrosewriting.com

Printed in the United States of America
Suggested Retail Price (SRP) $17.95

Lucky Brilliant is printed in Garamond

*As a planet-friendly publisher, Black Rose Writing does its best to eliminate
unnecessary waste to reduce paper usage and energy costs, while never compromising
the reading experience. As a result, the final word count vs. page count may not meet
common expectations.

For Jacob, Ethan, and Zachary

ACKNOWLEDGMENTS

My first novel has been a long time in the making. It would never have come to fruition without the encouragement of my wonderful friends. I want to thank Sharon Kurtzman, Diane Chamberlain, Elaine Orr, Nancy Young, Bernie Brown, Therese Fowler, Robin Miura, and Barbara Claypole White for their steady support over the years.

Thank you to Black Rose Writing for believing in this book enough to bring it into the world. I would also like to thank the independent presses and journals that have published my work.

Finally, I would like to thank my husband, Barry Peters, for his love and guidance in all matters of the heart and the page.

Lucky Brilliant

PROLOGUE

When the blue Volvo flew off the dark road and into the ravine, the canvas that Chase Brilliant had purchased for his daughter's Western Civilization art project slid forward like a ghost-white passenger and landed against the windshield.

A moment before he crashed, Chase's daughter, Lucky, appeared—green eyes, black wavy hair, heart-shaped face. Was this a dream? "Lucky!" Chase screamed as the car tumbled and smashed into an army of oak trees and evergreens blanketed with new snow.

The windshield shattered. The canvas, along with Chase's green Upward Mobility blazer, settled into a patch of snow and twigs.

The next day, a New Jersey state trooper discovered a hubcap and shattered tail light on the road. In the ravine he spotted a heap of burned metal. All that remained in the snow: a piece of canvas and a damp blazer. In the lower pocket of the blazer, the trooper found a man's wedding band inscribed *My Darling Chase / 8-90 / Alice*.

In another pocket was a velvet box containing an engagement ring. This puzzled the trooper most—that a married man carried an engagement ring. *Why,* he wondered, as he called in the accident.

ONE

I knew something was wrong.

I felt it in every raised goosebump on my arms. I paced from the piano room to the kitchen to the dining room, my mother's melodic notes following me. Outside, streetlights highlighted the plump snowflakes cascading like confetti at the end of a party. I was worried about finishing Mr. Harrington's history project on the French Revolution, but I had to get outside and taste the snow.

February. Spring was around the corner. I closed my eyes and imagined the pink flowers on the rhododendron bush in front of the house. It hadn't snowed all winter. As I passed the Steinway, my mother yelled, "Lucky, wear a coat!" I ignored her and shut the door.

Soft specks of cold touched my face and arms, melting on my lips. The flakes felt like a dog's tongue licking my face. I danced in a circle as I often did with my dad.

My best friend, Eva Mongelli, appeared. Only a row of low hedges separated our two houses on Evergreen Drive—we lived at fifty-five, Eva at fifty-seven. Brickville was a typical New Jersey suburb full of brick ranches and split-level homes built in the 1960s. School teachers, police officers, and gas station owners were our neighbors. My dad was a real estate agent; Eva's dad was the elementary school principal.

"Hey! It's snowing!" Eva said, spinning around, her patent leather boots reflecting the white. Dark oversized sunglasses, pushing back her straight black hair, rested like a band on her head. Eva loved to twirl and wear interesting shoes and clothes. I wore my usual jeans and T-shirt. Eva said I dressed like a boy, like her brother Silas, who was a year older than us. That night Eva wore a long black wool coat with a purple-and-yellow scarf loosely knotted around her neck. Her hair draped over the scarf and velvet collar.

"Why the glasses?" I asked her.

"Moon glasses. Very stylish, no?"

"No."

"Should we make snow angels?" Eva asked.

"We're getting too old to make them. You said so way back in middle school."

"I changed my mind." Eva adjusted her scarf. "Girls are entitled to, you know. Even tenth-graders."

We fell back on my lawn, moving our arms and legs, staring into the dark sky speckled with snow.

"It seems so far away, yet so close," I said.

"What? The snow?"

"No, the moon, silly. It makes me consider what's out there."

"Oh, man, Lucky. There's no moon tonight. You're losing it. Have you been talking to Mr. Kean again? Getting all philosophical on me?"

"He did give me some books to read. Camus. Kafka. I don't know why I feel so serious lately. Maybe I'm just worried about that darn project for Mr. Harrington."

A chill raced up my arms. It wasn't only the French Revolution project or the surprise snowfall. It was the same terrible feeling I got when I knew something bad was about to happen.

"You haven't finished it yet? You, Miss gets-everything-done-a-month-ahead-of-time?"

"Long story. I still have to paint my interpretation of the Women's March on Versailles."

"Painting. Your specialty," Eva said. "You'll be done in a New York minute."

"You got your project finished on time? Miss call-in-sick-on-the-due-date-of-a-project-and-hand-it-in-the-next-day?"

"Silas helped a bit. He was bored."

"You mean Silas did the whole project for you."

"More or less," Eva admitted.

"Wish I had a brother."

Eva jumped to her feet, grabbed my hands, and yanked me up. We ran down the street, the covered macadam shimmering like diamonds beneath the streetlights. We stopped quickly, sliding long imprints into the fresh snow. Then Eva drew a big heart with her heels and wrote *Eva and Sean, true love.*

"What happened to Peter?" I asked.

"History. Peter is so last month." Eva snapped her fingers and shimmied her shoulders as if hearing a tune inside her head.

"I can't keep track."

She wiped away the heart in two patent leather swipes.

"Here today, gone tomorrow," I said. That's the way that it was for Eva. But not for me.

"Such is love," she giggled.

"Who's getting philosophical now?"

We ran again, energized by the snow. But I stopped short, anxious.

"What's wrong, Lucky?"

"I'm okay. Just a stitch."

"Growing pains," Eva said. "Looks like my tiny friend is finally hitting her growth spurt."

"I hope so. It's not easy being the shortest girl in tenth grade."

"Well, it would definitely be harder being Harrison White, the shortest *boy* in tenth grade. Guys don't mind a short girl, but a short guy–forget about it."

"How do you explain Billy Watson?"

"There are exceptions. And he's not that short. And he's a wrestler, too."

I wrote my name with my sneaker, then watched the snow fill in the hollowed indentations. Another chill raced up my neck. Gone. I had the sensation that when the snow melted one day, I too would vanish. Shivering, I wrapped my arms around myself. Even though my best friend stood beside me, I felt suddenly alone.

Eva pirouetted away and waved goodbye, leaving swirls in the snow. I watched her go, then looked up at the black sky filled with flakes. Something was wrong.

I stood outside the house waiting for the headlights of my father's car. But the narrow stream of light never came. Over and over a voice in my head whispered, *Where is Dad?*

TWO

Mom's hands danced across the ivory keys of the Steinway playing Schubert's Impromptu in B-Flat. The Steinway was an heirloom from her late mom, my grandmother. Notes filled the piano room of our small ranch house on Evergreen Drive. Our Italian Greyhound, Monty, sat on the floor beside the piano bench.

I looked out the window. Once in a while, headlights shined and then vanished. I turned to Mom, who was staring at me. After thirty-two years at the piano, she didn't have to look down at the keys to play.

"Where's Dad? He should have been back already. It's eight and I don't have the canvas to do my painting."

"Well, you know how Dad is." She stopped playing and put on her soothing voice. "Always late. He'll get here."

"But he promised. And if I don't do this by tomorrow, I can't get an A. It's for my French Revolution project. The report's almost done. But I have to create the Women's March on Versailles."

"I tried to call him but his phone's out of range or something. If you want, I'll run out and get it for you."

"No. It's not only the canvas. Dad promised to help me."

"Lucky, it's so late to be starting."

"I did the pencil sketches and research. I told Dad about the project weeks ago but he didn't get it."

"He'll be here. He always pulls through in the end. He was late to our own wedding. Did I ever tell you that?"

In the framed wedding photo on the wall above the piano, Dad, handsome in his white tuxedo and black tie, stared at Mom. She wore a tentative smile, the scar on her chin erased by the magic of photo processing. Mom focused on the photo too. She touched the scar.

I turned back to the window, spotting headlights slowing down. But the car rolled past.

"It's Mr. Kean," I told Mom, then slinked into the kitchen. Monty followed me.

Mom returned to the piano, filling the house with Schubert. I put bread in the toaster, but after a minute the darn thing began smoking again. The appliances were breaking one by one.

Back in the piano room, Mom had stopped playing. I peeked in—she was looking at the wedding photo again. I'd heard the story a hundred times, how Mom couldn't believe Dad had chosen her when he could have had anyone. He proposed on stage after performing the lead in *Guys and Dolls*. After the second curtain call, the spotlight had shifted to Mom at the piano, who turned wide-eyed and pale. Then another spotlight illuminated Dad. He dropped to his knees and called out, "Marry me!" The mesmerized audience of three hundred leaned forward in their seats, silent, waiting for her response. When she said "Yes," the cast and audience broke out in cheers and whistles.

Dad jumped off the stage, knelt beside her piano bench, and slipped the diamond ring on her finger. The other actors and orchestra members huddled around them, bombarding the young couple with hugs and kisses and congratulations. One cast member appeared with two bottles of champagne. Corks ricocheted off the theater ceiling. The audience clapped, rising in a standing ovation.

When Mom asked, "Why me?" on their wedding day, Dad replied, "Why you? You're beautiful, smart, and levelheaded. I'm entranced by your music. I want to spend my life with you."

I loved the re-telling of their story. I looked away from the photo and back to Mom.

"He probably had a last-minute house showing," she said. "You understand how his clients are, demanding him at all hours."

She followed me to my bedroom. On my desk were preliminary sketches of my painting, women in long, colorful dresses holding swords, pitchforks, and axes. One played a drum.

"You're so talented. I can't even draw a straight line. Neither can your father."

I didn't look up.

"Sorry, sweetie. I'm not sure what happened to Dad. Looks like you made do without the canvas."

"Mom, I've got to finish this. Will you please go?"

"I only wanted to say goodnight," she said.

"'Night. Close the door."

She leaned down to kiss me. I pulled away. Yes, it was mean, but I couldn't help it.

After she left, I lay in bed remembering a phone call from a few weeks ago. Dad and Mom had gone out, but he had forgotten his phone. I found it on the kitchen counter. Instead of picking it up, I watched VIC flashing on the front. For some reason, those letters stayed in my head.

I finally drifted off to sleep, Monty dozing by my side, long after the clock blinked 10:00. Dad still wasn't home yet.

THREE

After getting dressed for school, I found Mom at the kitchen table, an empty plate in front of her.

"Is Dad here?"

"No, honey," she said. "I'm sure he's fine. He probably had a showing and stayed at work. With the snow and all."

I watched her pour orange juice into her coffee.

"Mom! What are you doing?"

She stopped mid-pour.

"You're worried. You're putting orange juice in your coffee."

"I know, Lucky," she said. "He's never stayed out all night without calling."

"So contact the police."

"I did. They can't do anything yet. They took my information. We have to wait."

"But what if something happened to him?"

"Nothing's happened. Now get your backpack. I'm sure he'll be here when you get home."

"Fine."

I turned away. She kissed my cheek. I grabbed my project, painted on old brown cardboard instead of a new canvas, patted Monty on the head, then left for the bus.

The day passed in a blur of classes and faces. I turned in homework, ate lunch with Eva, walked the halls like a zombie. I actually thought about leaving school, right past the front office and through the big glass doors, and running home. Was

Dad there yet? I pictured him sleeping on the sofa, Monty snuggled beside him. He would surely be there when I got back.

Somehow, I made it through the day and began walking home without waiting for Eva. At three o'clock I turned the corner to our street. The Volvo was nowhere in sight. I ran across the lawn. Inside I found Mom weeping on Mrs. Mongelli's shoulder.

Mrs. Mongelli whispered to her. Mom shook her head. Mrs. Mongelli walked away to the kitchen.

"Come here, sweetie," Mom said.

My face grew hot and sweaty.

"What is it? Where's Dad? His car isn't in the driveway."

Mom held my hand, patted the empty spot on the couch next to her. I wouldn't sit down.

She looked up as if searching the air for answers. As if she didn't want to open her mouth.

"I'm so sorry, Lucky. So sorry." Her face tightened. "He was in a terrible car accident. They found his Volvo. It burned."

My stomach lurched. A nauseous sensation rose in my throat. I yelled, "Why aren't you at the hospital? Why are you still sitting here?"

"There is no hospital." She turned away and wiped her eyes. "He didn't make it."

The air in the room disappeared.

"No," I said. "No. Daddy isn't dead. It's a mistake. Someone else is dead. Not Dad."

"Lucky, I wish it were someone else. But the police came this morning and told me the news. It's Daddy. Come here."

She stood, cradling me in her arms and hugging me so tight I couldn't move. My hands turned into fists and I began punching the air behind her back.

"Shhhh, shhhh, baby. It will be okay." She tried to soothe me as she had done when I was a child. But I didn't feel like a child anymore.

FOUR

The sun hurt my eyes when I finally woke the next morning. I'd cried myself to sleep with Mom next to me. I expected her to still be under the covers, but she was gone. Only Monty offered comfort. He kept nuzzling my hand with his wet nose. Wiping the crusty nightmare from my eyes, I was certain this bad news had been a dream. In a minute, Dad would traipse into my room humming "Oklahoma!" But I heard voices in the living room. The words *funeral, eulogy, sorry.*

Mrs. Mongelli sat in the living room next to Mom. She jotted down a neat list of to-do items to help prepare for Dad's funeral, gently asking Mom questions and recording information. I listened silently.

"Give me the list," Mom said, pulling the paper from Mrs. Mongelli's hand. "I want to make the calls, do all the planning. It will keep me busy."

"You sure? I'm happy to make the arrangements, Alice."

Mom said yes, then no. She picked up a glass of wine and swallowed the last drops. Mom occasionally drank at dinner parties and weddings. Once in a while with dinner. But I had never seen her drink wine this early in the day.

The doorbell rang. A neighbor delivering food for our grieving family would drop off the first of many tuna casseroles. Bad news spread quickly.

Mom kept herself busy the next few days. I stayed home from school, deciding that I should be by her side as she did the things she never thought she'd have to do. She made phone calls and sent in Dad's obituary to the *Jersey Tribune.* Tears sprang again while she sorted through pictures to choose for the death announcement. Finally, she decided on a photo of Dad smiling. It had been taken after one of his performances at the Brickville Community Theater.

The phone seemed attached to her ear. And with each call from a relative, theater friend, or one of Dad's co-workers at the realty office, Mom sounded more distant—colder, as if she were talking about a recipe or making a dinner reservation. As if she were talking about the death of someone else's husband and father.

It took Mom's sister to break through the cool exterior that she was attempting to wear. Aunt Robin, the family psychic, lived in Miami.

"Oh my God!" Aunt Robin said on the speakerphone, followed by a moment of shocked silence. "Alice, how are you? How is Lucky handling everything?"

"As well as can be expected," Mom said, looking at me.

"Horse manure. You don't sound right. Who's with you, besides Lucky?"

"No one. Well, Maria Mongelli came by at first. But I told her to go home."

"Are you nuts? You shouldn't be alone. There must be someone who can come over right now."

"People have been dropping off food. We're fine."

"Alice, look. Call your rabbi, a couple of temple members. You shouldn't be alone."

"I told you eons ago, we don't belong to the temple anymore. I'm fine."

"I'm on my way," Aunt Robin said. "I'll drive straight through. I should be there late tomorrow night."

I liked Aunt Robin. Mom called her predictions a bunch of hooey. She didn't believe that Aunt Robin actually had premonitions or talked to spirits. But I was glad that Aunt Robin was coming. I could ask her if she had predicted that something awful was going to happen.

And I could finally tell her that I also had dreams that came true.

•   •   •

The funeral home filled quickly to a standing-room-only crowd of mourners. Dad would have been pleased. Several of his friends and co-workers delivered humorous and heartfelt speeches. A dozen weepy middle-aged women gathered in a circle and shared vivid stories about Dad as a boy; they had attended the girls boarding school where he and his mother, the school nurse, once lived. At one point, Dad's theater friends gave him a standing ovation—his final one.

I wandered the room, my arms attached to Eva and Silas. From time to time, Silas put his warm hand on my shoulder. It made me feel peaceful.

Mom stared in a dreamlike state, clinging to Aunt Robin, trying not to faint.

Back at the house, two tables were pushed together to accommodate all the trays of food. Neighbors, teachers, and theater people packed the rooms. Laughter broke out occasionally. I knew the noise disturbed Mom, that people were eating and having fun as if nothing bad had happened. They would catch her staring and then the smiles vanished.

Mom grabbed my hand and took me to her room. Aunt Robin followed.

"It's the way it happened," she said, sipping wine.

"The crash, you mean?" Aunt Robin said, sitting beside her sister, her side of the mattress sinking beneath her heft.

"I imagined being at his bedside when I was eighty and he was eighty-two," Mom said. "Maybe he'd have a heart attack while on stage in the middle of a song. Or a stroke. I'd hold his hand and he'd say, 'You're the love of my life. I've been a lucky man to have you all these years.' He'd look into my eyes one last time, then drift off peacefully. I'd go the next day. Or the next year."

"Nothing is ever like we imagine it will be," Aunt Robin said.

"The Brilliant curse. Chase always talked about it. Both his father and grandfather were dead before they turned forty. That's why he said he had to pack in twice as much as most people did. He thought he'd die young. It's not fair. I'm a widow at thirty-seven. My daughter has no father."

Aunt Robin pulled me over.

"At least you have Lucky. And have you looked in the mirror recently? I wish I looked like you! You probably haven't given it a thought, but eventually you might want to get married again one day. You could pick any guy you want."

Why would Aunt Robin say something like that so soon?

"No one will ever compare to Chase," Mom said. "I don't want anyone else."

"Chase wasn't exactly perfect," Aunt Robin said.

Mom looked at me, then back at Aunt Robin. "What do you mean by that?"

"Oh, nothing. Nothing." Aunt Robin glanced at the photo of Dad that sat on the dresser. "I'm sorry."

She hugged Mom, then me.

"I want to stay, but the psychic hotline awaits me."

"I still can't believe you make a living that way," Mom said, sipping more wine.

"Someone's got to do it. It's like being a social worker. People need me. Anyway, it pays the bills."

Mom looked at the floor. "I can't go out there. All those people. They were Chase's friends. I wish everyone would simply go home. I'm so tired all of a sudden."

"Okay," Aunt Robin said. "I'll stay another day. I'll go out there with you. You just sit and drink a glass of wine and nod when people talk to you. They don't expect you to do or say anything. When they leave, you relax. I'll clean up. Tomorrow before I go, I'll do the grocery shopping, pay the bills. Whatever you need me to do."

"Thanks, Robin. I'm not sure what we'd have done without you here."

"Don't thank me. I'm your sister." She looked at me. "And your aunt. That's what family is for."

I squeezed Aunt Robin, happy she was staying the next day. I had a lot to talk to her about.

• • •

"Grab a drying cloth, Lucky. We'll get all these put away as a team."

Aunt Robin stood at the sink washing dishes.

"Can I ask you a few questions?" I reached for a casserole dish, then dried it with the kitchen towel.

"Shoot. All ears."

"What are your dreams like?"

"The psychic ones?"

"Yeah. Are they like movies? Like real movies you're watching? Then a day or so later, the story comes true?"

Aunt Robin stopped rinsing a serving tray and turned off the water.

"Are you having dreams?"

I nodded. She pointed to the table and we sat down.

"Yes," she said. "It's like a movie, in color, but I only see brief shots and hear certain phrases. Once I saw a man cheating on his wife, a friend of mine. He was in a hotel room whispering in the woman's ear. I couldn't hear her voice, only his. Another time I heard a scraggly dog whimpering. He showed up at my door the next day with an injured paw."

I nodded. My dreams were similar. In color and cuts of a film with only certain people talking.

Aunt Robin reached over and rubbed the top of my head. "You have it, my dear. The gift."

"I'm scared. I don't know if it's a good or a bad thing."

"It's a little of both. It can be good and bad."

I hugged her and we returned to the dishes.

•   •   •   •   •

The visitors stopped coming. The phone stopped ringing. The mailbox stopped filling with sympathy cards. Mom stared at her list, neat little check marks beside each to-do item. She crumpled the paper, opened a bottle of wine, finished it, and fell asleep. For days she slept, vaguely aware of my presence before or after school. I would bring her soup and tea. Every time she looked at me, she acted as if she were seeing a ghost.

FIVE

I hadn't cried at Dad's funeral. People kept saying "You're so brave" or "Keep being strong for your mom." But the truth was that I didn't believe that he was dead. Dad seemed larger than life—six feet tall, vibrant and funny.

First of all, the police hadn't found a body, just burned bones. And when the police lab tried to do its tests, confirming the bones really were his, they couldn't locate the remnants. Apparently, they were stored away somewhere, mislabeled or lost.

When I pointed this out to Eva, she said, "What about the green blazer?"

"He isn't the only man who has one of those. Lots of people work for Upward Mobility."

"But Upward Mobility isn't as big as one of the other places."

"It's big enough. The third biggest real estate agency in New Jersey. Dad told me."

"What about that piece of canvas?"

"Other people must have bought canvas that night. It didn't have my name on it."

"And the ring? The wedding ring?"

"Well, Mom says she saw it, briefly. But she was so shaken up, she didn't know for sure it was his. They haven't released the ring yet. Mom thinks they may have lost that too. It probably ended up in the same container as the bones."

We were walking Monty. He stopped to sniff the bushes. Eva took a deep breath.

"Lucky, you're upset. But get real. You're in denial."

Of course Eva was right. Probably right. I couldn't wrap my head around the fact that Dad was gone.

"What are you, a psychologist? It's not the evidence—the bones, the ring. It's more a gut feeling. I'm not insane, but there are times when I'm walking, I'm aware of his presence. Like he's alive. Right beside me."

Eva's eyes widened. "You are nuts. Look, Mom told me that grief does stuff to people. Look how together my father is. But when *his* father died, he couldn't sleep. He walked all night. Sometimes he didn't come home until morning."

I couldn't imagine Mr. Mongelli—the elementary school principal—feeling that way. Feeling that he wasn't in control.

"Your dad did that? He's so ... well, such a creature of habit. He wears the same color bow tie on the same day, right? Red on Tuesday, yellow on Wednesday."

"That's my point," Eva said. "Even he went a little wacko."

"I'm not wacko," I said.

But it was what it was. I didn't accept Dad had actually died, so I didn't grieve. I was sad, though. I missed him. My theory was that a thief stole Dad's car—or stole the personalized license plate ACTOR and put it on his own car. At any moment Dad would knock at the front door, a big smile on his face. He would hug me and say how much he missed me.

•   •   •

The first Sunday without Dad, Mr. Kean, my favorite neighbor, stood on our front stoop with his *Jersey Tribune*.

"Lucky, want to read the comics with me?" he asked through the screen door. Mr. Kean understood how much I enjoyed this Sunday morning ritual with Dad. We had started it when I was barely a toddler and continued, off and on, right into high school. It was one of those traditions neither one of us wanted to give up.

Mr. Kean tried to comfort me. The thought of reading the comics alone on the same gray couch that I had shared with Dad, our socks touching sole to sole, made my eyes itch. I wiped the moisture and nodded.

"Mom, I'm going to Mr. Kean's," I yelled, wondering if she heard, or if she was even awake. Mom hadn't left the house for days. Every night I slipped into her dark bedroom, checking to make sure she was breathing, and removed the empty wine bottle and glass. Mom would mumble something incoherent and turn toward the wall.

Mr. Kean and I sat in two rocking chairs on his porch. I wanted to laugh as Mr. Kean's slow, deep voice read *Family Circus, Marmaduke,* and *Dennis the Menace.* I imagined Dad's big feet pressing against mine. I floated, alone, lost in the rocking, in this new dark place without him. Absent the melodic laughter, I tried to hear his voice instead of Mr. Kean's baritone, but it was no use. Already I struggled to remember the rise and fall, the tone and texture of Dad's laughter. Would I forget what he looked like too?

It suddenly felt like I was falling. I stopped rocking and tried to focus on Mr. Kean, this kind man beside me. Beneath his wild eyebrows and behind his gold-rimmed glasses, his wide-set eyes scanned the comics page.

When he finished reading, I thanked him. He handed me the paper and nodded.

"Are you working for me Tuesday?" he asked. "There's a house full of dusty furniture in there."

"Of course," I said. The Keans asked me to work for them every week, cleaning inside or doing chores in the yard. I thought of the last time I had worked for them, more than a week ago, dusting the furniture in the hallway and the living room. Then, making sure I was alone, I turned the doorknob to the mystery room. Once again, it was locked. Mr. Kean had told me it was a private room and didn't need to be dusted. Still, when the Keans were in another part of the house, I tried to turn that knob. Each time I found it locked.

Back home, I sat on the couch and closed my eyes, trying to recall Dad's voice. A chill ran up my neck when I felt the weight of a hand on my shoulder.

"Mom?" I said to the empty room.

She was nowhere in sight.

"Dad?" I whispered.

Only the rustle of newspaper blown by the vented warm air answered back. I reached down, crumpled the funny pages, and threw them as hard as possible across the room. They landed behind Dad's photo on a side table.

"Nothing funny here," I muttered.

SIX

A week after the funeral, I returned to school, thankful for the distraction provided by the daily routine: classes, friends, and art lessons with Baxter Geller in his studio on Main Street. At home, I was surrounded by sadness and silence—no noise except Mom yelling one afternoon after school.

I had gone to her bedroom door and peeked in. Propped up in bed, Mom talked on the phone, her face red, her voice growing louder by the second. The scent of bitter coffee saturated the room. A green Upward Mobility coffee mug sat on the bedside table.

"I don't understand why you haven't begun to process the claim," Mom said. "I left four messages."

There was a pause. Her eyes met mine.

"Yes. That's right. Chase Brilliant. It was a 2003 Volvo. Yes, I'll hold."

Mom shook her head, then handed me the phone as she drank coffee. The Muzak version of 'It's My Life" played through the receiver. When the music stopped, an actual voice said, "How may I help you?" I gave the phone back to Mom.

"Lapsed? Lapsed? No way ... no, I don't pay the bills. My husband does. Did."

Coffee spilled, staining the comforter brown. Wrestling with the tangled sheets, Mom tried to climb out of bed.

"Are you kidding me? We paid insurance for ten years! Because we missed two months, you canceled our policy? We didn't file any claims for ten years! None at all! You can't do this! You can't do this to me!"

She took a deep breath.

"Don't tell me to calm down. You're doing me a favor by returning my call? What do you want, a medal? Don't you get it? I have no money. None. Do you see why I'm upset? My husband died in that Volvo you were supposed to insure and now you're telling me it wasn't? I have no car and no money. Thanks for nothing."

Mom threw the phone across the room. It clanked and bounced on the floor. As if suddenly remembering I was there, she looked at me, then at the phone. Swollen-faced, tears dripping down her cheeks, she said, "I'm sorry, Lucky. Sorry you heard that. Don't worry. I'll work this out."

"Mom," I said. "We don't have any money? How come? Dad worked. Didn't you save anything?"

"Lucky, everything will be fine. Don't you worry."

On the nightstand was a stack of bills hand-delivered yesterday by the receptionist from the Upward Mobility office. She had dropped off a box containing Dad's possessions—photos, framed community awards, various knick-knacks he kept on his desk, and a thick stack of mail. Mom hadn't opened the bills; she continued to pile them on the table, a confused look on her face.

What would it be like to have no money? Shaky, I left the bedroom, the earth trembling beneath my feet.

• • • • •

Brickville High School filled me with new worries. Everyone was aware of my sudden fatherless situation and wanted to talk to me about what happened. In a daze I walked around the school. I thought the routine of chemistry, geometry, Spanish, lunch with friends, culinary arts, Western civilization, and English would be a welcome distraction. If I pretended to appear normal, perhaps I would begin to feel normal inside. But friends and strangers alike knew about Dad's death. Brickville was a town of only ten thousand. My classmates had been together since kindergarten. Kids who didn't usually look my way now stared uncomfortably, pity in their eyes. When I returned their stares, they turned away. Only Eva and Silas maintained eye contact with me.

My teachers were kind. Ms. Albert, my math teacher, unexpectedly put a hand on my shoulder after class the first day back and said, "I lost my own dad when I was nearly ten. If you need to talk, I'm here." Most teachers said "Sorry for your loss" or nodded. Even the grumpy ones like Mr. Harrington managed a smile.

But I wished nobody knew, especially the other kids. The way some of them looked at me, I wondered if two heads had sprouted from my shoulders.

"Everyone's acting so odd," I told Eva.

"They don't know what to say."

"I wish they'd simply ignore me. I wish I was invisible."

"It'll pass. It's like movie star gossip. Britney Spears shaved her head, got a tattoo, and checked herself into rehab. A couple months from now, no one will remember any of it. And she's a star. You're just a fifteen-year-old from the suburbs."

"I guess."

"Remember when Ginnifer Park's mother died of cancer when we were in third grade?"

"No."

"See? You've already forgotten."

Eva was trying, but it didn't help much.

"Look at this," I said, handing my hero essay to her. The week before Dad died, I had submitted it to the *Brick Literary Journal*. The prompt was to write about a personal hero. Of course, I had written about Dad pursuing his dreams, not giving up his goal of becoming an actor.

"You won honorable mention," Eva said.

"I don't care. Look at her comments."

So sorry about your dad. This is a lovely tribute to him.

"It's a pity award."

"She meant well," Eva said. "Honestly, what could she say?"

I grabbed the essay and slid it inside my backpack, wishing my sadness could be stored away so easily.

SEVEN

On Wednesday I walked from school to Baxter Geller's studio for my art lesson.

Mr. Geller's studio was on Main Street above Happy's Soda Shop. If I lived there, I'd probably weigh three hundred pounds from eating sundae after sundae. Mr. Geller's apartment had four rooms: a kitchen, a bathroom, a bedroom, and a big living room with a fold-out sofa for when foster kids stayed with him. The rest of the living room was studio space, one big open area with high ceilings and lots of light.

The scent of ground coffee, hot fudge, and French fries filled the studio, mixing with the odor of turpentine, oil paint, and a crock pot of Mr. Geller's stew. My stomach rumbled. I craved a lime sherbet cooler but the twenty-dollar bill stuffed in my pocket, from my housework at the Keans' last week, was only enough to pay Mr. Geller. When I had asked Mom for the check to pay for my weekly lesson, she shook her head, saying something about overdrawn accounts. She said I should skip art class until things improved. I couldn't wait until I turned sixteen so I could get a real job, like waitressing or working at the art supply store.

I pointed out that I had already missed one lesson and the big Brickville Fair was coming up at the end of July. I wanted to enter the art show this year and I needed to work on my paintings. The winner received five hundred dollars. We needed the money.

Mr. Geller had hung a new painting that took up an entire wall. It looked like an unraveled Slinky at sunset. The image seemed to slip right from the canvas and spill onto the paint-smeared hardwood floor. One wall displayed canvases of student paintings. Mr. Geller gave lessons to only five students. He was selective.

Five years earlier, Dad and I had shown up with a portfolio of comics. Mr. Geller asked, "Why do you draw, Lucky?"

"Because I have to," I told him. "I wouldn't know what to do with myself if I wasn't drawing. I even draw in my sleep."

He asked one other question: "Do you dream in color?"

I nodded. He walked us to the door and looked at my right hand, which was callused from drawing with pencils. He said, "You can start on Wednesday. One-hour lessons."

The five years had flown by. I set the twenty-dollar bill on the wooden crate that rested against the wall. Mr. Geller smiled and said, "Cash?"

"Is that okay?"

"That's fine."

His gray hair was pulled back in a neat ponytail. He wore a tie-dye shirt, as usual. I loved that shirt: it reminded me of a sunset in utopia, with splatters of purple and yellow, but mostly bright orange. Against his pale skin, the vibrant colors brightened his complexion. He also wore cargo shorts that hung below his knees all the time, even in winter. And he always wore ankle-high boots. Dried paint coated the hair on his legs.

I once saw a photo of Mr. Geller in an old *Art Today* magazine from 1985. He looked young, about thirty, but he'd become famous overnight, dropping out of the Rhode Island School of Design his sophomore year. By twenty he had his first gallery show under his belt. An art critic called him the "Picasso of the Baby Boomer Generation." A year later, his paintings sold for fifty to one hundred thousand dollars each. The Metropolitan Museum of Art acquired two, as did a museum in Chicago and another in Paris. By twenty-three Mr. Geller was worth millions. Then he gave it all away, saying the money and fame interfered with his creativity. That propelled his fame even more—he appeared in every art magazine in America and throughout Europe. He even landed on the cover of *Time*.

Now Mr. Geller lived like a pauper. And there was no Mrs. Geller, merely a school of foster children who paraded in and out of the studio. Emanuel, a sixteen-year-old, was painting in a corner of the studio when I arrived.

"Hola, Emanuel," I said, practicing my Spanish.

"Hola, Lucky. Cómó estas?"

"Bien."

Emanuel laughed at my attempt to speak Spanish and then pointed at his canvas.

"So what do you think? Te gusta?"

"Me gusto. Reminds me of a nightmare," I said, his dark-winged creatures sending chills up my spine.

"What are we working on today?" asked Mr. Geller.

"I want to start a series for the fair. It would be great to win a prize."

Mr. Geller smiled. "Nothing started and already you want a prize. The prize doesn't matter, Lucky. The art matters."

"Still, I thought it would be cool to do a series. A comic strip series in oil paint."

He nodded. "Been reading Crumb again, I see."

Mr. Geller and I both had a taste for Robert Crumb, known as R. Crumb, and his wild cartoons. I had learned about him from Dad.

I sat on a stool, my feet not touching the floor, and began opening paints. There was no furniture to speak of, just two paint-splattered wooden stools, three crates, and built-in shelves lined with art books. Jazz filled the room from an ancient portable radio, electrical tape wrapped around the dial and antenna. Emanuel swayed back and forth. He dabbed his brush in paint, then stroke by stroke added to his winged creatures. Like most of the kids, he seemed happy to be there. I wondered what happened to Emanuel, to all of them, when they left the studio.

Mr. Geller opened a window next to my work space. He lit a clove cigarette, the sweet smell drifting toward me. Cars passed in the street below. Men and women strode quickly on the sidewalks. A boy walked a small barking dog.

As I painted, my whole body relaxed—neck, arms, fingers, even my toes. And with each stroke of the brush, I felt more alive. I became the lines and the swirls of color. All my worries flowed into the paint: Mom staying in bed, the bouncing checks, the loneliness, the grief. The sweet smell of Mr. Geller's smoke rose into the March air.

EIGHT

Exactly one month after Dad died, I had one of my dreams—the kind that seem like they might come true. Like the ones Aunt Robin constantly had.

My latest dreams were always in the form of a newspaper article, with big black headlines and black-and-white photos. I had told Baxter Geller I dreamed in color, which was true, except for the newspaper dreams.

The latest headline: *Pharmacist Killed in Bank Robbery*. The article told how Mr. Johnson, the local pharmacist, died from a gunshot wound during a robbery at Brickville Savings & Loan on Main Street. *Mr. Johnson was sixty-eight years old. He leaves behind a wife, Betty, two sons, and four grandchildren*, according to the dream newspaper.

I woke in darkness, breathing as quickly as if I'd run Monty around the park on a hot summer day. Whenever anyone needed medicine, my mother and I would go to Brickville Drugs, two stores down from the bank. Mr. Johnson, a short, plump man with kind eyes and thick white hair, always said, "Lucky! How is the prettiest brunette in Brickville doing today?" Then he'd reach into his big white pocket and hand me a yellow or blue gumball. One day I stopped by the store and delivered a drawing of him in his pharmacy jacket, standing behind the counter, smiling. When he held the drawing, his eyes grew teary. My nine-by-twelve picture still hung on the wall behind the cash register. He'd even framed it.

I had seen Mr. Johnson a few days before when Aunt Robin was visiting again. She and I had filled a prescription so Mom could sleep at night. Apparently, the wine she drank wasn't helping her.

I wanted to do something about the horrible dream, but it was three a.m. Even Mom was asleep, the pills having done the trick. I got a drink of water and returned to bed hoping for peaceful, dreamless sleep.

.　　.　　.　　.　　.

Mom used to be the first one up but since Dad died, she stayed in bed while I dressed for school.

"Good morning," I said, setting coffee on her cherry nightstand, moving an empty wine glass. Every morning, a tiny pocket of air formed in my throat, questions hovering in the morning light: Will Mom wake up? Is she still breathing? Out of habit, I would lean over the sheets and listen for proof of life: What will I do if she doesn't wake up? Who will take care of me?

Then her legs would move and I could finally take a deep breath.

"Hi, Lucky," she said, yawning. She stretched her arms toward the swirling ceiling fan. Mom said her temperature ran hot—it had to do with hormones. Dad always wore layers in bed but Mom would kick off the sheets, saying she suffocated in the heat. I noticed that she still slept on one side of the bed as if expecting Dad to take the empty side during the night.

Yesterday morning I had found a covered lump beside her. My heart raced; I briefly thought it might be Dad. Then I pulled the covers away revealing Monty, curled up warmly beneath the blankets. Maybe because the blinds were pulled shut, or maybe from the dust swirling in the room, but the once-bright flowers on the comforter appeared dark and dead.

I flicked off the TV. Mom had gotten into the habit of falling asleep listening to the news or late-night talk shows.

"Thanks for the coffee," she said, lifting the steaming cup to her lips. Her other hand rubbed the right side of her head as if trying to push away pain.

I thought about telling her my dream about the bank robbery and Mr. Johnson, but she probably wouldn't want to hear about it, not with everything on her mind. Nonsense, she would say.

Instead, I asked her if she had money for my lunch since the Keans hadn't paid me yet.

"Sure," she answered. "Check my purse. Take what you need."

"I did, Mom. You only have a dollar."

"Oh. Well, then make something."

"There's one slice of bread, or I would."

"Well, go to the old tzedaka box in the living room. There might be a few dollars in there."

I felt guilty taking the three dollars from that wooden box. Once a year, Dad used to empty it, then he and Mom would go to the Brickville Soup Kitchen and donate the money. They liked to imagine all the down-on-their-luck men who would eat for days with the donated money. Giving always made them feel good. Dad had even convinced the director of the community theater to donate all the proceeds from *The King and I*, *Cabaret*, and *The Music Man* to the soup kitchen.

But today the hunger in my stomach was as wide as the Grand Canyon. The casseroles that once lined the freezer shelves were gone. The pantry was empty except for macaroni and cheese, a jar of peanut butter, a box of spaghetti, some stale Cheerios, and outdated cans of pinto beans. Neighbors no longer knocked on the door with plates of sugar cookies and piping hot ceramic dishes holding chicken or stew.

After eating a slice of toast, I said goodbye to Mom. I spilled dry dog food into Monty's metal dish, refilled his water, and scratched his neck. The nightmare still gnawing at me, I decided to go to Eva's house.

NINE

The Mongellis' house was the biggest one on the block. It should have been, since six people lived there. Eva's mother looked ten years older than Mom on account of the four kids, according to Eva. She said taking care of so many children made her mother's hair turn gray. Though Eva encouraged her to dye her hair black, she refused, so it remained gray and wiry on top.

When she was younger, before marrying Mr. Mongelli, Eva's mother modeled. I never would have pictured it if I hadn't seen the framed *Vogue* photos on the wall of the new addition to their house. The photos didn't even look like her mother but they looked like Eva, or how Eva might look in a few years. Now Mrs. Mongelli had permanent, scowling wrinkles, as if someone had pinched her skin near her mouth and eyes and they remained that way. It was like she had an annoyed look on her face all the time. Eva said it was mainly on account of the twins, five-year-old Braxton and Brandon, aka *The Destroyers*. They sent their mother over the top.

And then there was the lightning incident with Silas.

I heard high-pitched yelling, as usual, on the other side of the front door. The twins were fighting already. Silas was probably sitting quietly, reading or playing video games. Sometimes I thought that Mrs. Mongelli would be happy if the little ones became silent like Silas. She flung open the door as she did every morning, her hair a mess. She wore an oversized, misbuttoned dark shirt, one side hanging longer than the other. Red stains dotted the pocket as if a tomato had exploded. Had she gotten into an early morning food fight?

"Come in, Lucky," she said.

I cautiously stepped inside, nearly tripping over another group of Home Shopping UPS boxes stacked in the foyer, the tile hard beneath my sandals. The energy of the house woke me. Each room was painted a different color: eggplant purple in the living room, ketchup red in the kitchen, sunshine yellow in the family room. I caught a scent of marinara and my stomach growled. Even though I had eaten that slice of raisin toast, Mom hadn't made dinner the night before. I was still hungry.

Eva twirled into the kitchen in a new spring ensemble, a beige-and-red floral skirt with large roses, a silky red top, and matching Manolo Blahnik's, all courtesy of her wealthy grandparents during a recent shopping spree in New York City. Her hair was slicked back, the loose part swirling in black circles with each turn.

"You like?" she asked.

"Yes, I like," I said, admiring her shoes. "Dorothy? You going back to Kansas?"

Eva clicked her red shoes three times. "Oh, no, darling. Didn't I tell you? Grand-mama is taking me to Paris in August."

"Wow. Paris. That sounds like fun."

I smiled to hide my jealousy. Mom and I wouldn't be taking a vacation anytime soon. And the only vacations we'd ever taken as a family had been a few days at the Jersey Shore. Point Pleasant or Manasquan.

"The fashion in Paris," Eva said. "Think of it! Me at Hermès! I'll have to ship my purchases home."

Eva's wardrobe already included two Hermès scarves that cost a bundle. I smelled the marinara and eggs in a pan on the stove. My stomach rumbled again.

"Hungry?" asked Eva, sitting at the table sipping water.

"A little." I eyed a plate of pastries and English muffins, butter rivers melting into bread valleys.

Eva handed me a paper plate. I grabbed a muffin and ate it quickly, then took a cheese Danish. Eva ate nothing. Silas smiled at me from across the table between bites of his croissant. I smiled back, then whispered to Eva, "I've got to talk to you."

"Go ahead. Silas might listen but it's not like he'll tell anyone. Unless he writes one of his notes."

I had never told Eva about my dreams before. I debated how much I should say.

"I had a terrible dream."

"What about?"

"A bank robbery. Here in Brickville."

"So?"

I glanced at Silas, then back at Eva. "I'm afraid it's going to come true."

"Don't be silly," Eva said. "Dreams don't come true. Only in the movies."

"I know," I said. "It's silly, but I can't stop obsessing about it. What should I do?"

"Nothing," Eva said, crumpling her plate into the wastebasket. "See if it comes true, I suppose. But don't tell anyone else. You don't want people to think you're out of your mind. It's getting kind of late. We'd better get going."

Though I didn't agree with her, I was glad she changed the subject.

"Are you walking to school in those?" I asked, pointing at her bright red shoes with their two-inch heels.

"Practice, practice. Fashion over pain. Heels are important. They lift your bottom and change the whole look of your chest."

I looked down at myself.

"Well, once you get a chest," Eva said.

I grew warm, a flush rising in my cheeks. I glanced quickly at Silas, who grinned. In fact, my old bras no longer fit. I needed new ones. It seemed like I woke up and there they were. Not that anyone else would notice. Eva wore a C-cup. Next to her I still looked flat-chested.

Grabbing my backpack and one more pastry for the road, I followed Eva out the door and we began the half-mile walk to school.

"So why did you get so freaked out about your dream?"

We were passing the Keans' house. I waved to Mr. Kean, who rocked on the porch. Mrs. Kean was nowhere in sight.

"A bank robbery's a big deal," I told Eva.

"On Main Street? In our little town? No way will that happen."

Cars whizzed by. One slowed down and an older boy, his mop of blonde hair hanging out the window, whistled at Eva. She lifted her chin and smiled.

"A person dies," I said. "Mr. Johnson. The pharmacist."

Eva's red shoes clicked to a halt. "What? Are you pulling my leg, Lucky? Have you gone bonkers? You're under a lot of stress from your dad's death. You saw all this happening in your dream?"

"Yes," I said. "I was reading a newspaper. It's what the article said. I'm completely scared it's going to happen."

"That would be bizarre, Lucky, if we could predict the future."

As we approached Brickville High School, Eva shifted the conversation to boys, mainly which seniors she had a crush on. And which upperclassmen had a crush on her. I had less interest in the subject, but I listened because that's what friends do. Most boys acted immature, like eighth-graders. The only boy I ever talked to sat at the Mongellis' kitchen table that morning. Even though he didn't talk, Silas looked and acted like the seventeen-year-old high school junior that he was.

And he was a good listener.

TEN

Dad had wanted to call our new dog "Sir Barks-a-Lot" because he didn't bark at all. He said the Italian Greyhound would be a walking irony. But Mom and I shook our heads and said that was a dumb name. So we agreed on Monty, as in *Monty Python's Flying Circus,* Dad's favorite show.

By the time I was ten, I could sing "Eric the Half-a-Bee" and recite the entire "I Want to File a Complaint" skit. Dad had said that comedy played an important role in my education and I wouldn't learn it at school. He explained that only intelligent people understood humor. Dad argued that comics were the true geniuses in society and that a person with a sense of humor would always have a job and friends.

"I need to learn to be funny?" I had asked, slightly doubtful. My teachers hadn't mentioned any of this.

"Well, it's gotten me out of a lot of sticky situations," Dad said.

"Like what?"

"Tickets. Getting towed. Those kinds of things. And it can get you a great table at a restaurant or a nightclub when they tell you there aren't any left."

That seemed like a good thing to know, so we watched *Monty Python* reruns over and over. Dad always took the part of Eric Idle and I took whoever was left. He told me that when the show ended its run, he wore black and spoke with an English accent for a week. After the *Monty Python and the Holy Grail* and *Life of Brian* movies were released on video, he watched them day and night.

Naming the dog Monty made him smile.

Now, Monty was the best part of coming home from school. Mom would still be in her room when he greeted me at the door. I would take him outside immediately, then after I put a little food in his dish, we'd go for a walk. Dad would be pleased.

Today as we strolled the neighborhood, I thought about how Dad and I loved the comics. When money became tight, Mom had canceled cable television, the bottled water delivery service, and our annual trip to the Jersey Shore. Then she canceled the newspaper.

When Dad protested, Mom said, "We only throw it away anyway." But I joined Dad in pouting. We loved the comics. Dad's favorite was *Blondie*. He thought Blondie looked like Mom in a cartoonish way, except Mom's hair was straight and her eyes were two different colors, one blue and one green.

My favorite cartoonist was Crumb. His work didn't appear in the newspaper; Dad bought his books and I insisted he read them to me. Even though I didn't always understand what his comics said, I appreciated Crumb's artistic talent. And I felt a special bond when I found out that Crumb and I were born on the same date—August 30. I figured it was a sign. We both loved to draw. As my pencil created characters and scenes on paper, my real-life worries dissolved, the problems melting away. When I grew up, I wanted to work for Marvel Comics or, better yet, create my own comic strip. Years later, when the paper arrived on Sundays, I would sit with my children and read the comic strip that I had created.

But Mom won the battle over the newspaper. We became the only house on the block that didn't receive it. She said I should read it at the library or keep up with the news by watching television. I teased her, saying she must be the only parent in Brickville who encourages her daughter to watch more TV.

"Oh, I'm not worried about that," Mom said, tousling my hair. "You rarely watch it."

She was right. Between school, art lessons, working for Mr. Kean, and hanging out with Eva, I had little free time. Still, I missed the newspaper. For as long as I could remember, on Sunday mornings Dad would tickle me awake and say, "Time to get up, funny girl. The funny pages await you."

I'd rub the sleep crud from my eyes and giggle until my belly hurt. Dad had a magic power: he could make anyone laugh. It seemed like even Monty smiled in Dad's presence.

Each morning throughout elementary school, before he dressed in his green Upward Mobility realty blazer with the embroidered logo of a couple ascending a golden staircase—before he left for the day to show houses to young couples who were starting out, or to big families whose three-bedroom homes were bulging at the nail-gunned seams with infants and toddlers, strollers and toys—Dad and I would take turns reading the comics on the couch. We would skip the soap operas because they were too boring and *Doonesbury* because it was too political. Dad hated politics and didn't vote, but I thought he would have made a great politician because of all the people who knew and loved him. He even had wonderful hair. And he always smiled, shook hands, and held other people's babies. Had he run for mayor of Brickville, he surely would have been elected.

When my feet grew tired of balancing against the bridge of Dad's feet, I'd hug my knees real tight, making a flannel tent. In the kitchen Mom flipped chocolate chip pancakes even though strawberry ones were my favorite; we didn't eat strawberries because of Dad's allergy. When he was six, Dad nearly died after eating strawberries at a picnic. Once in a while Mom would join us, smiling at the funnier comics. She liked *Peanuts*, especially when Schroeder played the piano.

Dad and I always finished reading the comics in laughter. My voice was kind of deep for a girl, and when I had a giggle-fit, even Mom, who was usually serious, joined in. But her laughter wouldn't last long. She would quickly put her hands over her mouth, silencing herself, as if embarrassed by joy.

Since Dad's death there had been no laughter in the house. There had been no music, either. Before that day Mom's students had come to piano lessons every day. Around the holidays, "Jingle Bells," "Rudolph the Red-Nosed Reindeer," and various Chanukah songs rang out in the piano room. Years before, Mom had abandoned her dream for me to become a child prodigy and searched elsewhere for talented musical hands. I used mine for drawing.

Sometimes I liked hearing Mom's students play. Other times, it was painful. One day, trying to solve algebra equations for the first time, I thought that if one more student hit a wrong note, I would pull the waves right out of my hair. "Twinkle, Twinkle, Little Star" and "Yankee Doodle" played so often in the house that the songs vibrated in my head late at night. If I never heard "On Top of Old Smoky" again, I'd be a happy person.

The more advanced students practiced "Raindrops Keep Fallin' on my Head" from *Butch Cassidy and the Sundance Kid*, one of Dad's top ten movies. I'd seen it twice. Something about Dad reminded me of Paul Newman. Perhaps the glint in his eye.

After the students left, Mom would play Chopin's preludes and etudes. I loved listening to them as I finished my homework and drew my comics.

The past month, though, the Steinway sat heavy and quiet in the music room. One day as Mom lay in bed, I asked her if she was going to play anymore. She shrugged and looked sad, as if she might cry, so I didn't ask her again.

Now I wished that Monty did bark so there would be noise in the silent house.

ELEVEN

When I got home from school, Mom was sleeping in the darkness of her bedroom, the cold, black coffee on the table half-full.

"Mom. Mom. Wake up. It's three-thirty."

"What? Lucky? You're home."

"Mom. Shouldn't you get up?"

"I'm so tired," she said, rolling to her side away from me. "Let me sleep."

That night I tossed in bed, my stomach growling. For dinner I had scooped out peanut butter and the remaining spoonful of grape jelly. After finding stale crackers in a drawer, I spread peanut butter on them, but my hunger didn't go away. Beneath the pink comforter, Monty wiggled against my leg. The house felt cold for March. When I had asked Mom to turn up the heat, she pulled the covers to her chin and said, "Do you have money to pay the heating bill? It's March. It'll warm up soon."

"Dad always kept it cozy warm."

"Maybe that's why we don't have any money."

"But I'm freezing."

"Then wear leggings to bed. Take an extra blanket from the linen closet."

Zipped inside my down jacket, I shivered beneath the blankets even wearing the leggings and my favorite purple sweater. After Aunt Robin sent it to me for my birthday a year ago, Eva had shrieked. She read the tag and informed me "Givenchy," lifting one impressed eyebrow.

I didn't care where the sweater came from, only that it was my favorite color and very warm.

All night long I heard odd noises. The wind blew; a branch scratched against the house over and over. Falling in and out of sleep, I dreamed of a newspaper floating, birds carrying the sheet of black-and-white paper above the house. The paper vanished, and the white sky filled with a swarm of birds that changed into a color comic strip of Dad crashing his Volvo. I saw his face, heard screams, smelled burning tires. His hands floated and reached for me. He yelled "Lucky!" and I sat up, my name echoing in the room, my skin wet with sweat and fear despite the chilly air.

Then another sound. Not the wind or a branch, but a high-pitched squeaking. I jumped out of bed and followed the noise toward the attic. The stairs were pulled down from the ceiling; a crack of light slivered the otherwise dark hallway. I lifted the folding stairs back into the attic, then shuffled to the bathroom. Wiping sleep from my eyes, I sat on the toilet. The towel bar across from me looked strange, so I rubbed my eyes again. What was that dark stain on the tan towel? Were my eyes playing tricks? A sock? A splotch of dirt?

I sucked in my breath, resisting the urge to scream. A bat! Right there on the towel! What was it doing? Were there others? I moved slowly and quietly. Pulling up my leggings, I opened the door and stepped into the hallway, the whole time keeping my eyes on the creature. Then I slammed the door, grabbed towels from the linen closet, and jammed them against the space at the bottom of the door to block the bat's exit.

I bolted to Mom's room. She lay in bed, a lump beneath the covers. Another empty wine bottle sat on the table and a pile of forwarded mail littered the floor. On the front of one envelope in block print were the words NOTICE OF FORECLOSURE. I wasn't sure what that meant, but I understood it was bad.

"Mom! Wake up! A bat. There's a bat in the bathroom."

"What? Why are you waking me up?" she slurred, her tongue thick with sleep and wine.

"Mom, help me. Get the bat!"

"Tomorrow, Lucky. We'll get a bat tomorrow," she said, rolling away from my voice.

If Dad were here, he'd help, I thought. He'd find a net or a container and take care of it. I hated spiders and bees. When one found its way into my room, Dad would wake at any hour and save me.

But Dad wasn't here, so I had to be the hero. I closed Mom's door and found Dad's big leather gloves, the ones I'd given him for Chanukah, in a closet. Holding them to my nose, I tried to smell traces of him, but they only smelled like leather. I took a deep breath, picked up the towels, and cracked open the bathroom door, trying not to shiver. The bat hadn't moved. Was it sick? Rabies? I slowly cradled the brown creature with the gloves. It didn't try to fly; it barely twitched one wing. Was there an entire colony waiting in the attic? Was this sickly one, the outcast, kicked out of the colony? Had this bat lost a loved one too?

Holding it glove-handed in front of me, I walked slowly through the hall and kitchen, careful not to let the creature loose. I elbowed the handle on the back door, then pushed it open with my foot. The creature's dark eyes gazed up at me. Outside, I set it down on the cold grass, sadness heavy in my chest. My throat closed up. My whole body shook. Tears fell like dew freezing onto the blades of grass. I went back inside and sat on the couch, hugging myself, until the darkness slid away and the sun came through the window, warming my face.

I threw the gloves in the wastebasket on top of the empty peanut butter jar, cracker box, and coffee grinds. The gloves reminded me of the bat and Dad's hands. Afraid of rabies, though, I had to trash them.

After dressing quickly, I grabbed Monty's leash and took him to the front yard. He spun in a circle, then lifted his leg near a bush. I wondered if the blooms would turn yellow instead of pink from Monty's pee.

We walked around the house to the back. I hooked Monty to his chain and searched for the bat, but it was gone.

TWELVE

During Western Civilization with Mr. Harrington, right before lunch, my stomach growled so loud that Eva laughed. I sank in my seat, hands crossed over my belly, trying to muffle the noise. Something other than growling rose in the pit of my stomach: dread. The question had been gnawing at me all morning long. Would the dream come true? Would the shooting at the bank happen today?

My fear increased when Principal Glass announced on the intercom, "The school is on lockdown effective immediately. Teachers, please keep your students in class. Make sure the doors are locked. No one is to enter or leave the building."

"And I was gonna leave early today," said Quinn, a red-haired boy with pimples dotting his forehead. "I have a doctor's appointment."

"What for?" asked Brad, his seatmate. "Zit zapping?"

Brad doubled over with laughter at his own mean joke. Eva kicked the back of his chair and said, "Idiot. Have you looked in the mirror lately?"

Quinn grinned at Eva and blushed.

Eva leaned toward me. "What's this all about?"

Everyone shifted in their seats, talking. Mr. Harrington clapped his hands and silenced the chatter.

"Folks, read chapter nine in your books. And take notes. We're still having a quiz in two days on the French Revolution." Then he sat at his desk and read a magazine.

The newspaper from my dream still fresh in my mind, I wondered if it was all happening at this moment. I remembered that the robbery had taken place late in the morning, according to the article. The hands on the large black-and-white clock above Mr. Harrington's desk read 11:05.

The air grew hot and thin. It smelled like sweat and Mr. Harrington's heavy cologne. I felt crowded by the desks and the chairs and the walls. Images of Mr. Johnson, the pharmacist, filled my head.

I turned to Eva and whispered, "Bank robbery."

"How would you know?" Eva shifted in her seat.

"My dream. Remember the dream I told you about? The bank robbery. Didn't you listen to what I told you yesterday? Why do you think we're on lockdown?"

Eva frowned. "Remember when it happened in sixth grade? When that guy escaped from the Rahway prison? All the schools were on lockdown. And they found him two streets away from the prison, nowhere near here."

"How could I forget? I missed my art lesson. Dad talked his way into the school and got me out."

With the exception of the prison escape, there hadn't been a newsworthy event in Brickville since the train derailment in 1998. It filled the *Jersey Tribune* pages for a week. A depressed ticket-seller had been served divorce papers through the customers' ticket window. He put three suitcases, his wife's boxed china, an antique sewing table, and his wedding band on the tracks one morning before sunrise. The 6:20 train bound for New York flew off the tracks. Two passengers died; ten more were injured. Since then, an old security guard patrolled the tracks from the Brickville Station to Metropark.

Eva and I ignored Mr. Harrington's assignment. I couldn't concentrate with the fire-breathing dragon of worry. Meanwhile, Eva passed notes to Chad, a blonde-haired boy with blue eyes who was class president and had long runner's legs. Kids complained about missing lunch. They talked and played hangman. Somebody pulled a deck of cards out of their backpack. Finally, at two o'clock, Principal Glass came back on the intercom: "Thank you for your patience. The lockdown is over. Since parents are eager to pick up their children, there will be an early release. You may be dismissed now."

Outside, nervous and relieved parents rushed to find their children. Collective sighs of relief and chatter swirled in the parking lot. A procession of hugs followed. I spotted Silas standing beside Eva's mother, then I searched for Mom. She was nowhere to be found.

Mrs. Mongelli squeezed Eva tight until she complained, "Mom, puh-leeease!"

Then Mrs. Mongelli put a hand on my shoulder and asked, "Are you girls okay?"

"What's the big deal?" Eva demanded, hands on her hips. She tossed her thick hair that, in the afternoon sun, shined blue-black like a doll. Silas shrugged.

"Is your mother here?" Mrs. Mongelli asked me, scanning the sea of heads.

I kicked a pebble and looked toward the circular track in the distance. I wanted to run away. Cars looped through the lot past others that were parked at odd angles and far from the curb. Finally, I looked up at Mrs. Mongelli's dark, bloodshot eyes, detecting a shadow of sadness or pity.

"We still don't have a car," I said. "Unless she walked here. But I don't see her."

I wondered if Mom would ever drive again. Mr. Kean had offered his Cadillac convertible lots of times so Mom could get groceries or run other errands. But Mom always refused his offer. I didn't think it had anything to do with her being uncomfortable with borrowing his car. When Aunt Robin had visited, Mom refused to drive her car, too. Even before Dad's accident, Mom had been a nervous driver, gripping the steering wheel tight with both hands, not allowing conversation while she drove. When Dad was alive, he drove all the time.

Shortly after Dad's accident, Mrs. Mongelli took Mom to see the totaled Volvo. Mom had come home with a look of terror on her face. Mrs. Mongelli said that her eyes were big and her skin was pale. I asked Mom about the car, but she refused to say a word. She quietly shook her head and vanished into the piano room. Her hands grazed the keys but no music came. She simply sat there, staring at the keys.

I kicked another pebble. Eva picked up my hand and swung our arms back and forth, something she did whenever I was tired and nodding off in class, or when she wanted to snap me out of a funk. She'd been doing this since third grade.

"You can come home with us, Lucky," Mrs. Mongelli said. "But let's get moving. Mrs. Sullivan is picking up the twins at the elementary school. She won't be able to handle them for long."

When we were settled in the SUV, I asked the looming question: "What happened, Mrs. Mongelli? Why did they lock down the school?"

"Let me guess!" Eva interrupted. "Robbery at the bank on Main Street."

Mrs. Mongelli gasped. She nearly hit the car bumper ahead of us, slamming on the brakes so hard the tires screeched. She whipped her head around. "Who told you?"

"What? You mean I'm right?" Eva's smile vanished.

"Yes, I'm sorry to say. There was a bank robbery and—well, you'll hear it on the news anyway. A hold-up."

My hands trembled. Eva and I looked at each other. A sour taste filled my mouth.

"Was anyone hurt?" I asked.

Mrs. Mongelli jammed the brakes again, stopping short at a red light. We all jolted forward, then our heads snapped back.

"Sorry about that, girls," she said. "I'm a bit distracted."

Silas raised both arms, then pointed to himself as if to say, *What about me?*

Mrs. Mongelli hesitated for a moment. When she started talking again, there was something familiar about her voice. It was exactly how Mom's voice sounded before she told me about Dad.

"I don't know all the details," she began. "I turned off the news and came here as soon as they announced the lockdown was over."

The light turned green and the vehicle moved forward.

"One person was shot. A sixty-eight-year-old man from a store right on Main Street. It doesn't sound good."

"Mr. Johnson," I blurted out.

"Where did you hear that?" Mrs. Mongelli asked, looking at me in the rearview mirror. "Did someone tell you, Lucky?"

I shook my head. "No. Nobody told me. I just know it's him. He's sixty-eight. We were in the drugstore on his birthday a couple weeks ago."

"Well, it could be anyone," she said. "Let's wait. Whoever it is will likely be fine. Getting shot doesn't mean you die."

But I knew better. I had read the article; the details had unfolded in my dream. And even though I felt terrible about the robbery, excitement broke through the shock. I could foresee the future before it happened. As one side of my heart sank for Mr. Johnson, the other side pounded with the question: Would I have another dream that foretold the future? This question grew into another: Could I change the future and keep bad things from happening?

And this: Could I have stopped my father from going out on February 10th?

THIRTEEN

I found Mom in bed after Mrs. Mongelli dropped me home.

"Lucky? Why are you home? Early dismissal?" Her eyes moved from the photo to the red digits that flashed 2:15.

"Mom, you should get up, turn on the news. There was a lockdown because of a robbery on Main Street. Somebody was shot. The robber escaped so they locked down the school."

Her eyes narrowed and her mouth turned down. "Come here."

She hugged me tightly. It felt like being crushed by a crazy person desperately holding on to the edge of a cliff. I tried to pull away.

"My God, Lucky. I'm sorry you had to go through that. I'm so sorry."

"Well, you should get out of bed. Do something," I said, then left the room, feeling alone.

I flicked on the news for information about the robbery, but the press conference was still an hour away. I walked Monty, then went to Eva's house. She sat in bed in her lilac-painted room paging through *Vogue*, cutting out her favorite dresses, tops, and purses.

"Hey, Lucky." She motioned me to sit on her Yves Delorme duvet cover, purchased at Le Bon Marche in Paris by her grandmother last spring. I loved Eva's room. The bay window, with a built-in seat covered in tiny lilac-and-yellow flowers to match her desk chair and duvet cover. The fancy thick molding with a whipped-cream border halfway up the wall. A newly hung valance and lilac blinds custom-ordered from a window-covering store in New York.

The door to her walk-in closet stood open, so I got up and explored. It felt like being on a *Lifestyles of the Rich and Famous* rerun that Mom and I watched.

Cashmere sweaters and tops in different colors and fabrics lined the shelves. A built-in dresser made of whitewashed wood was set into the wall.

"Can I try on those pants?" I asked, spotting a new pair of Prada jeans.

"You don't have to ask. Do a fashion show." We'd been putting on fashion shows since elementary school. Usually Eva was the one modeling her new outfits.

With my mind filled of thoughts about Mr. Johnson, I needed a distraction. The fashion show began. I started with skirts then moved onto pants, surprised to find everything loose-fitting. The jeans slipped off my hips. Odd. Eva was a size four and I was sort of a size four. Her pants always ran several inches too long for me, which was still true, but the waist that always fit a bit snug now hung loose.

"Eva, this can't be a four," I said, checking the label.

"Same as always. Four." She got off the bed, set the magazine down, and stuck three fingers beneath the fabric at my waist.

"You've lost weight. I thought you looked different."

I shrugged. I didn't obsess about weight or appearance the way Eva did.

"Are you dieting?"

"If you count skipping breakfast and dinner as dieting." I looked away, not wanting to answer the next question.

"Why aren't you eating?"

"They're a different cut. They fit weird. I don't want to do a silly fashion show." I yanked off the jeans and hung them on a fabric-covered hanger. Eva sat on the window seat staring at me in a strange way. I sat next to her and changed the subject.

"I've been thinking about my dream," I said. "What good is it having dreams that tell the next day's news? That is, if more come."

"That would be awesome. You could prevent things—bad things—from happening."

"Speaking of bad things, mind if we check the news? I want to hear the latest on the robbery. There's supposed to be a news conference."

In the living room, Silas sat in his usual spot on the velvet purple-and-beige floral couch. He watched the news and wrote in a notebook. Even though the house was cool, my cheeks radiated heat. I smiled at Silas and he smiled back. He had really nice lips. They weren't thin like other people's. Why had I never noticed this before? The twins threw a tennis ball in front of the couch. The next throw hit me in the leg. Silas shot them a look; they grabbed the ball and ran outside.

Mr. Johnson died at 3:20. His photo appeared on the screen. I flinched. I held my hand over my mouth, suppressing a cry. Eva shrieked. In the photo, probably from ten years earlier, Mr. Johnson's hair appeared full and he wore a big smile. Why hadn't I done something? The question screamed again and again like a siren. My head throbbed with the knowledge that I might have prevented his death.

I got up quickly and ran home, afraid I'd start crying and not be able to stop.

As I walked up the front steps, I heard a thudding sound. On the dirt beside the door lay a blackbird, its neck slightly bent. Its glazed eyes stared up at me.

"Poor baby. Didn't see the window?" I said, touching its slick feathers. How could death be so soft? I thought about germs and disease, but only for a second before picking it up. I brushed off the dirt from its wings, cradled it in my hands, pressed my lips against the blackness. My tears spilled onto the dark feathers. They would not stop. So much death occurring in such a short time, more than one person could bear. A light breeze blew and suddenly the bird's eyes moved, then the feathers fluttered. *He's alive!*

I set him back down and thought of the bat. Was this a sign? Maybe Dad was not actually dead. I watched darkness pass over the yard, a plane whose shadow resembled a large bird. For some reason I thought of Mom, of shadows and darkness and nights in the house.

In the first month after Dad died, I often heard Mom crying at night through the paper-thin walls. Only the bathroom separated our rooms. It seemed as though she was mad. When the phone still worked, she would call Aunt Robin after drinking wine. One time she said, "He was a fool. No life insurance, no savings. I've got bills piling up that I can't pay. And there were other things."

Sometimes the squeaking music of bats began. After a while the high-pitched noises almost comforted me. More than Mom's sobs or late-night conversations, anyway.

I lay in bed wondering what those other things were that Mom talked about to Aunt Robin. Did I have the wrong person? Maybe Mom wasn't talking about Dad; maybe she was talking about a neighbor or her own father. I was pretty sure that my grandfather had given Mom the scar on her chin, but I didn't understand how or why. Whenever I asked her about what happened to her father, her hand touched that thin white line on her chin, or one hand swept over the scar on her left leg. Her eyes looked away as if she saw an image she didn't want to see. A shadow of some sort. Then she would change the subject.

Once Aunt Robin hinted at it. She said something like, "Why are you still angry at our father? He's gone. Forget about him."

So I tried not to listen to the phone calls through the walls or to the pillow-muffled crying. And when the phone stopped working, there were no more calls at night. Only sobs.

FOURTEEN

The funeral for Mr. Johnson took place two days after the robbery. News cameras lined the walkway to the funeral home. Having no desire to be on the news, I stood away from them. Eva, of course, smiled for the cameras and even stopped for an interview with the Channel 4 reporter. The camera loved Eva. I figured she would become a model like her mother had been.

I begged Mom to come with us, but she said she wasn't up to another funeral. She told me to represent the family and send her condolences. The funeral was standing room only. I squeezed in front of Mr. Kean and found two empty seats. Ten minutes later Eva sat beside me, her face aglow, gushing to relay the details of her interview.

"Not my first time on TV, but my first speaking part," she smiled. True to form, Eva wore a sleeveless black Dior dress, adorned with a strand of glowing pearls, and a knit bolero jacket that covered the tops of her arms. On her head sat a large-rimmed black hat, a sheer black veil skirting her eyes and nose.

Mrs. Johnson was seated in the front row beside two grown sons and four grandchildren. Several people spoke from the podium: the mayor, the other pharmacist, the two sons, even the adorable tiny granddaughter who referred to him as Grampy Johnson. She cried when she said, "He gave the best hugs and made people all better with his medicine."

Afterwards, Eva and Mr. Kean drove back to the neighborhood together, but I told them I wanted to walk. Mr. Kean looked at me with concern and said, "Are you sure?" I told him I was. He understood. "Walking thoughts," he winked, right as usual. He understood my need to churn through this tragedy.

A few blocks from the funeral home I stopped at an intersection and waited for the light to turn. Across the street I spotted a man wearing a Mets cap, much like the hat Dad used to wear on his days off. It was pulled down to cover his hair and shade his eyes. He also walked like Dad—a strong, confident stride and straight posture, but not as fast.

"Dad?" I yelled, straining to see. The sun had faded and the sky seemed suddenly gray. It wasn't time to cross; the walk light flashed red. Following the man with my eyes, I pressed the button over and over. Cars sped by. Finally, the light changed and I ran across the street, passing men and women in business suits, people delivered home from jobs in New York by the evening trains. The man with the Mets cap was a thin blob blurring in the distance. He turned down a side street and vanished. I ran, nearly knocking down a man in a blue suit, racing to the corner where the stranger had turned. But he was gone. To the left were houses; straight ahead was the theater where Dad had starred in many plays.

Was he still alive? At Mr. Johnson's funeral I'd been afraid to look in the coffin, but I finally did. His skin was pasty. No smile, no personality. When I saw him, I knew for certain that he was gone. If only I could have seen Dad's body, touched his hand, his face, then I would know–for sure–that he was gone too.

When I gave up searching for the man in the Mets cap and began walking home, Silas appeared. He brushed away a dark strand of his wavy hair. His smile revealed perfect white teeth. When had the braces come off? I grew warm. Eva once told me what it was like to French kiss. I pictured kissing Silas this way. Lowering my eyes, I spotted books. In one arm he carried four books from the library–all science fiction, Ray Bradbury and H.G. Wells. Silas said nothing, but his presence both relaxed and excited me.

"Silas, can I tell you something?" He nodded. We kept walking. "I think my dad might still alive. Do you think I'm wacked?"

Silas shook his head and smiled.

"I keep seeing a guy with a baseball cap. It's like he's following me. And they never found a body. I honestly feel like he's not dead. I understand that I'm upset. In denial, like Eva said. But why do I keep asking all these questions?"

Silas shrugged. We stopped beneath an old tree. He moved the hair away from my face. It felt as if no one else existed. There was the tree and Silas and me. He looked into my eyes as if he were trying to read my thoughts. Next thing I knew, his lips touched mine. They were soft and moist. I opened my eyes. We both smiled. He held my hand, and that's how we walked all the way home. I wanted to dance and shout to the universe. There were no words to describe this feeling except happiness. Delightful, joyful happiness.

Thunder sounded out of nowhere and Silas squeezed my hand. I asked him if he thought it was going to rain. He pointed at the darkening sky, to a cloud sliding past. Since being hit by lightning two years earlier, Silas had become obsessed with the weather. Eva said that he watched the Weather Channel late at night when he had trouble sleeping. But since the lightning strike, I noticed a peacefulness in him. A light glowed behind his green eyes, as if heaven had sent down a light that now lived inside him.

FIFTEEN

I read in a book that the odds of being struck by lightning were one in a million. Two years earlier, when Silas was fifteen, he became that one.

It was July. Our neighborhood block party was winding down. Parents sat on folding chairs beneath a rented open-sided tent. Soda filled plastic cups. Beer bottles stood half-empty.

Suddenly a rumble of thunder shook the street. Dad's head angled up, studying the ominous sky. The Mongellis, the Sullivans, Mom and Dad, Mr. Kean—everyone voiced a version of "Kids, time to go inside. A storm's coming."

But no one seemed in any rush. We kept playing volleyball, ignoring the danger, the mysterious dark force that might chase others away, but not us. We believed our fast-growing skinny legs could outrun anything.

Silas chased the volleyball into his front yard. Earlier in the day, barefoot, he had stepped on a bee, then yanked out the stinger and returned to the game.

He reached the ball, turned to Eva and yelled, "Catch!" Before he could throw it, a loud crack of thunder snapped across the gray sky and rain started falling. Eva danced across our yard and opened her mouth wide, her tongue stuck out to taste the large drops. Then, in an instant, the rain changed to hail, pelting us with pebbles of ice. That's when a second bolt flashed like the open hand of God. Silas flew through the air and landed ten feet from where he'd been standing. A strange burning scent mingled with the hail and rain, the freshly mown grass and smoldering barbecue coals.

Silas lay on the lawn. Blood dripped from both ears. His hair was burned partially off in a bald line, a reverse Mohawk. Red streaks, like a severe rash, covered his arms.

The volleyball was shredded on the grass beside him next to a broken tree. The bark had been seared off the trunk.

Adults dropped their plastic cups and beer bottles and ran toward Silas. Mr. Kean arrived first, squeezing through the circle of kids. Eva knelt next to him, screaming, "Silas! Silas!" Mr. Kean moved her away and leaned over, listening. Then he pinched Silas's nose and breathed into his mouth. Dad had called 911; we heard the sirens getting closer. By the time they arrived, Mr. Kean had Silas breathing again. They carefully placed him on a backboard, restraining his head and neck. Mr. Mongelli climbed into the ambulance with Silas. Mrs. Mongelli followed with Eva in their car.

The rest of us stood there in the drizzle, the scent of burning oak filling the wet yard as the sirens faded in the distance.

Eva told me how lucky Silas was to be alive. Nausea, dizziness, sleepless nights, even a few seizures followed. He had lots of tests: PET, neuropsychological, CT scans, MRIs. And though his back hurt and sometimes his legs, Silas recovered faster than anyone had imagined.

But we all understood how that bolt of lightning changed Silas. Before, he'd been full of life. Hyperactive, a risk-taker. Since the incident, he had slowed way down. He'd become more deliberate, an introvert, as if the zap of lightning had rewired his personality. The doctors said Silas was like a computer—everything inside looked fine, but when you rebooted it, there was trouble with the operating system.

And the biggest change of all? Silas lost his ability to speak.

The Mongellis joined a support group for parents of children who suffered life-changing medical events. Mrs. Mongelli gained two sizes. And that was the last block party we had on Evergreen Drive.

SIXTEEN

Mr. Kean began dropping the Sunday paper at our house on Monday mornings in time for breakfast. I always flipped to the comics. Beginning with the top left, I worked my way down to the bottom, lingering at *Family Circus* and *Blondie*. It was a great way to start the day—a little art and humor.

If I had time after school and homework, I'd draw my own versions of my favorites, changing the dialogue, drawing in Eva or Silas. Sometimes I'd go over to the Mongellis and work alongside Silas. He would draw too, mostly landscapes incorporating extreme weather conditions–tornadoes, floods, lightning. One image he recreated again and again was that oak tree, its bark burned off by lightning. I'd draw Dad's Volvo careening off a road, his superhero body flying, hands reaching out above the ground.

Six weeks after Dad died—I had accepted it, hadn't I?—and the week after Mr. Johnson's funeral, I started reading the obituaries. The world of the dead had been a far-off place that didn't concern me. Suddenly it did. Two deaths in three months, and death had opened up like a canyon that had butted up against our yard forever, only I now noticed it sitting there beyond the bushes. I wanted to close my eyes to this horror film, but I had to watch at the same time. Dad had named this type of thing the *looky-loo factor*. Whenever traffic slowed to a standstill, the culprit being a minor fender-bender on the side of the road, every driver slowed to stare. They obsessively had to look.

And that's the way it was for me with the obituary pages. Suddenly I had to look. I couldn't turn away; in fact, I started drawing portraits and caricatures of the newly dead. I scanned for names, ages, occupations, causes of death. Mainly, though, I searched for survivors. Who were the ones left behind? I was, after all, a survivor. How many others were there like me, children without fathers? One day a Mr. Flynn died unexpectedly in his home. He was forty-four, leaving behind a six-year-old daughter, Cindy, and a two-year-old son, Malcolm. After carefully cutting out the photo of Mr. Flynn, who had thick, wavy hair like Dad's, I folded and tucked the obituary in my jeans. The viewing would take place on Main Street at seven that night.

· · · · ·

I walked Monty, filled his water dish, then realized the dog food bag was empty. After finishing my geometry proofs and Western Civilization chapters, I went to Mr. Kean's house to work. He was reading a book on the second step of his porch instead of his usual rocking chair.

"Hello, Lucky," he said, removing the unlit pipe from his mouth. "Here to work?"

I nodded, then looked away. "I know it's not Friday, but could I get paid for just the work I do today?" I kicked a stone into the grass. It vanished, concealed by long green blades.

"Sure," he said. "Want me to pay you for the whole week? Sort of an advance?"

"How much does one of those big bags of dog food cost?"

"Why? Is that what you plan on doing with your windfall?"

"Well, yes," I said, shoving my hands in my pockets.

He pulled out his wallet and handed me a twenty. "Here. This should do it. And consider it a tip, Lucky, not your pay. For doing such a fine job."

"No, you don't have to do that, Mr. Kean."

"I want to," he said, sticking the pipe in his mouth, going back to Socrates.

I swept the porch, pulled weeds, took out the trash, wiped away cobwebs in the upper corners of the porch ceiling. Mrs. Kean wandered into the yard, lost in her own little world. I didn't even wave anymore. I wondered what she saw in that world. In her usual spot, near the stump of a tree, she raised her arms to the sky. A V-formation of birds flew overhead, and her arms slanted up into a V as well. Did she think she was a bird? I imagined Mrs. Kean flying up and away, her curly white hair blowing free, her loose, fleshy arms flapping in the wind.

After a minute Mrs. Kean turned around, walked back up the steps, and stopped for a moment to look at her husband as if trying to remember who he was. A familiar glimmer lit her dark eyes. She smiled and placed a hand on his cheek. Surprise registered on his face. He put his hand over hers.

"Dorothy?" he said.

Mrs. Kean pulled back her hand. "She'll be home soon," she said.

Mr. Kean nodded. Then his wife vanished into the house. He moved from the steps to a rocking chair and opened his book, but it didn't look like he was reading. After a few minutes he finally turned a page.

I wanted to sit with Mr. Kean for a while. I could cheer him up. When I was blue, he always read stories to me or told funny stories about his own childhood. I dragged the trash to the curb, propped the broom in the corner of the garage, and sat in the rocking chair beside him. He put the book on a side table, pulled the unlit pipe from his mouth.

"Don't you have dog food to buy, dear girl?"

"Yes, I do. But I was cleaning up and realized you've never asked me why I'm called Lucky."

"Oh. Well, I assumed your parents appreciated how lucky they were to have you," he said, looking towards the sky, following a bird's flight with his eyes.

"I suppose that was part of it. My dad always said he wanted a gaggle of kids, but after they had me they stopped. Something about my mom getting sad after I was born. But I was a lucky kid. Once I found a gold wedding band at the beach when I was two, digging with a plastic shovel in the sand. I always found change and dollar bills in parking lots. My real name is Lucy."

"I know that," Mr. Kean said. "Your mom and dad were Lucille Ball fanatics. One of their first dates took place at an *I Love Lucy* festival. Your dad told me that story years ago."

"Yeah, but my name changed after Dad and I went to one of those fortune-tellers in Atlantic City when I was five. Mom was visiting Aunt Robin in Florida and Dad took me out of kindergarten."

I told Mr. Kean the rest of the story. He rocked back and forth, his eyes darting from the sky to me.

• • • •

We had passed several neon-lit casinos and mom-and-pop shops with their ocean-themed flip-flops and racks of T-shirts with large signs: *2 for $10!* Shirts with a choice of iron-on decals and sayings, an arrow with the words *I'm With Dummy* or

She's My Better Half. Further down, a legless woman sat in a wheelchair beside a big dish holding change and dollar bills weighed down by a rock so they wouldn't blow away. The woman's dark eyes met mine. I wondered if she dreamed about growing fins and a tail, becoming a mermaid and swimming away from her wheelchair and the Atlantic City boardwalk.

Dad said, "Don't stare, Lucy." He repeated that when we passed old skinny men with wrinkled, leathery skin carrying signs that said *Will Work For Food* or *Vietnam Vet.* One was missing an arm. They looked lost, hungry, unloved.

"Look at the ocean, the sand, anything else," Dad said.

"But why are they here?"

"For money. For the view."

After throwing stale bread over the boardwalk's edge for the seagulls, Dad led me into one of those fancy casinos. It looked like a castle that belonged in a foreign country—India or Egypt. Slot machines flashed and clanked and whistled. I wanted to stop and pull a lever, but Dad maneuvered me away from the noise into a café where a grandmotherly-looking woman with high white hair seated us at a small table. She took our order and walked away. Dad grabbed a piece of paper and a pencil.

"It's a game called Keno. Like the lottery. Pick five numbers from this sheet."

I pointed at the numbers and said, "10, 21, 32, 44, 53."

"Great job, Lucy. Now we give it to the lady and wait. Look up there at that big board with the numbers. If ours match the ones that light up, we win."

A skinny woman with a large chest and a very short skirt came over and smiled at us. She took the Keno ticket along with Dad's money and said, "Good luck."

The table had crayons for kids. I turned over my paper placemat and colored. Suddenly, Dad yelled, "Lucy, you did it! You won!"

I looked up from my drawing. "Can I get a piece of cake then?" I asked, pointing to a framed photo on the table of the seven-layer cake called Chocolate Sin.

"You stay right here. Order the cake. I'll be back in a second."

Dad returned to the table all smiles, patting his shirt pocket.

After lunch we walked along the boardwalk again. It felt warm for May. An ocean breeze kept moving my hair into my eyes. Dad put his arm around my shoulder and turned me toward a booth. A blue-and-yellow sign flashed *Fortune-Teller* in purple letters.

We walked through a beaded curtain. At a little desk sat a woman dressed in long, gauzy gold fabric. Her black hair hung down to her waist. Dark mascara made her eyes appear like sapphires. I stared at the mole beneath her nose. Bright beaded necklaces draped her neck like an upside-down rainbow. A gypsy, I thought.

She pointed to a chalkboard that listed the fortune options and prices, gold bangles jangling on her wrists. They sounded like wind chimes.

"You like your palm read? Tarot cards? Special today. Twenty dollars for both."

Then she winked at me.

"I'll add in a fortune for the young princess. Free."

I giggled. Dad nodded, and we followed the gypsy woman into a smaller back room. A tiny round table sat in the center. The fortune-teller wiped my chocolate-smeared hand, then turned it over. She smiled.

"You, my princess, are one lucky girl. Magic and laughter and a happy path. An artist. That smile will lead you to the pot of gold at the end of the rainbow."

She let go of my hand and stared at Dad.

"My turn?" he asked. She nodded and held his palm. Her face shifted. The smile vanished and her blue eyes narrowed. She shook her head, then dropped his hand as if it were suddenly too hot to hold.

"Little princess, will you wait in the main room? There's a crystal ball on the desk. You may gaze into it. And there's a candy dish. Help yourself."

I ran out through the purple curtain. Sitting by the crystal ball and chewing a piece of saltwater taffy, I heard whispers but couldn't make out the words. After ten minutes, Dad came out of the room. His smile was gone, which was unusual for him. He always smiled.

Dad grabbed my hand and we left in a hurry. He remained quiet. Looking out at the ocean, his shoulders slumped as if a heavy anchor weighed them down. We walked on the beach for a while. Next to a shell I noticed a shiny object. I dug a little and found a silver money clip with a five-dollar bill. I held them up and Dad smiled again.

"Your name is officially changed today. From now on I'm calling you Lucky," he said, picking up a broken shell and touching it to my forehead.

That day I felt like the Princess of Atlantic City. Like the luckiest girl in the whole world.

•   •   •   •   •

"That's a great story, Lucky," Mr. Kean said, stopping his rocker. "But I still like the name Lucy."

"Me too. Honestly, I may have used up all my luck when I was little. Do you think that can happen? If great things occur before a certain age, the luck all vanishes later?"

"An interesting idea. Many people believe in balance. They think we're responsible for making things happen with the positive or negative energy we give out to the world. And it can be a self-fulfilling prophecy."

"How do you mean?"

"Like if you expect to fail, you will make yourself fail."

"Do you think Dad died because he expected to die young like the other men in his family?"

"Another interesting thought."

"I've got to go, Mr. Kean. Time to feed Monty. Thanks for the pay."

"Bye, Lucy-Lucky. By the way, you haven't used up your luck. We shape our own destinies."

Mr. Kean could be right. I waved and walked quickly to the Stop Mart at the corner. My stomach grumbled. I grabbed a package of Twinkies and a big bag of dog food, then handed the clerk the twenty-dollar bill. She gave me back a quarter and two pennies. Outside I dropped the bag and ate the Twinkies in about four bites. Then I shouldered the dog food and struggled down the street under its weight.

Near home Silas appeared. I was happy to see him. He easily took the bag and put it on his broad shoulders. Already five-ten, he towered over me.

"What do you think it feels like when you die?" I asked him. Silas could hear perfectly fine even though he couldn't respond. He tilted his head to the left a bit, considering the question. Then he shrugged, shifting the weight of the bag on his shoulders.

"I've been thinking about it," I said. "Death, I mean. I wonder if it's like whatever you felt when you were hit by lightning. It must have been awful. I hope my dad wasn't in pain. Mr. Johnson, either. I can't bear to picture them suffering."

Silas nodded. We walked on silently except for the rush of passing cars, the chirping of birds in the trees, and one low-flying plane.

SEVENTEEN

The recently deceased Mr. Flynn lodged in my thoughts. His folded obituary in my pocket whispered to me throughout the day. At dinnertime I peeked in on Mom, who, as usual, slept in the dark room. A bowl of pinto beans remained uneaten on the side table.

In the kitchen I found a jar of old green olives in the back of the refrigerator. I nibbled a few as I sat at the kitchen table and drew. Energy pumped through my fingers. I filled the blank paper with the images parading through my head. I outlined the Volvo leaving the road, midair. I drew the snow and the full moon. Above the car an exaggerated, muscular hand reached down. Then I added the rest of the body—it was me in a Wonder Woman suit, an "L" etched on my chest. In real life I was tiny and slim, but in the drawing I was big and strong. In the next frame I reached out my rubbery, expandable arms and saved Dad, grabbing the car before it flipped over and caught fire.

In my daydreams that's how it ended. My nightmares revealed a different outcome. In those dreams I was small, far away and powerless, unable to stop the crash and the fire. I would hear Dad calling my name through the smoke and flames. Then, silence.

Over and over I told myself that if Dad hadn't driven to the store to buy canvas for my project, he would be alive. I wanted to move the calendar back to February 10. I wouldn't ask him to buy the canvas; I would beg him to stay home.

It was my fault. I was to blame. Not only for what happened to Dad, but for what became of Mom, too. That's why I took care of her. If it weren't for me, she would still be playing the piano. She would still be seeing her friends. She wouldn't be hiding in her room all the time drinking wine and sleeping.

I looked at the drawing for a minute. Then I picked it up and ripped it to shreds. Nothing helped. Nothing.

I threw away the empty can of olives and unfolded the obituary.

·   ·   ·   ·   ·

Wyndham Funeral Home was about six blocks away. I walked there in one of Mom's black shirt-dresses, using a thick leather belt to create a waist. The dress should have reached below my knees. Instead it swirled around my ankles.

A sign outside the front doors said Flynn, Room 2. I followed the other grieving family members and friends inside. An arched doorway opened to a room of cherry wall panels and rows of folding chairs. Warm light emanated from alabaster wall sconces. At the top of the high ceiling, thick ornate molding added to the formality.

The coffin, a long mahogany box, took center stage up front. The lid was raised, a soft-looking creamy fabric poking out. I saw the profile of a dark-haired man inside. He appeared fake, almost plastic, like the mannequins at Macy's. From ten rows back where I sat alone, he looked like Dad.

My heart raced. I tried to catch my breath. Mr. Flynn wasn't an old man. He was in his forties. Dad had died before he turned forty. Mr. Flynn wore a dark blue suit and a green tie. Dad's best suit, the one he wore to weddings and dinners, was blue and pinstriped, exactly like Mr. Flynn's.

In the front row of chairs, a young girl in a green satin dress with a large bow cried inconsolably. Suddenly she ran from her seat to the casket and screamed, "Wake up, Daddy, wake up! Don't be dead!"

Her mother tried to console her, but the little blonde girl wiggled away, darting toward the back of the room. Reflexively, I stood and followed. She ran into the bathroom. I found her sobbing on the tiles, her green dress draping her knees and forming a circle on the floor.

I knelt next to her and put my arm on her shoulder. Her mother came in and stood next to us.

"It's okay," I said to the girl. "I lost my dad, too."

The girl looked up at me. Long curled lashes blinked above her blue eyes. "You did?"

"Yes," I said. "Not long ago. And it stinks. It really, really stinks."

I looked at her mother, then back at her.

"What do you think I do when I get upset about it?"

She shook her head.

"I draw silly comics," I said, pulling a piece of paper from my dress pocket. I handed her the picture of a dog with floppy, oversized ears, large paws, and a curly tail. "The sillier, the better."

The girl took the drawing. "What's the dog saying?" she asked between sniffles, pointing to the empty bubble above the dog's head.

"He's saying, 'Take that, death. I'm not afraid of you! Bark, bark, bark.'"

She turned the picture over. On the back the dog was biting a hooded figure. Above were clouds, stars, and a dark-haired man with angel wings.

"Is that Daddy?" the girl asked. "Is he in heaven? Is he an angel?"

Her mother nodded at me.

"I think so," I said. "He's floating around with his angel wings. He's showing you that he's happy. That he's okay. And he wants you to be happy, too. He wants you to be with your mom and the rest of your family. They need you to help them say goodbye."

The girl hesitated for a moment.

"It's okay," I said. "You can have it."

Her mother pulled her up from the floor, touched my shoulder, and mouthed *Thank you*. I sat there for a minute, then got up and wiped off the black dress.

The sky had surrendered to darkness. Stars flickered and cars zoomed past. I began walking home. After a block I heard coughing behind me. I turned around, but no one was there. Goosebumps bloomed on both arms; I tried to rub them away.

A few minutes later, across the street, I saw a man walking in the same direction I was walking. He wore a Mets cap. I let him get ahead a few paces, then looked both ways and crossed the street. By the time I came to the next intersection, he had turned the corner and was gone.

EIGHTEEN

Eva invited me to spend Friday night at her house. I looked forward to a big Italian dinner with the Mongellis. My mouth watered at the scent of the lasagna. Even the assault of noise from the twins brought a smile to my face. I looked around for Silas. Every day since the kiss, Silas had slipped letters into my locker at school. I devoured his words. Whenever we passed in the halls, our hands touched.

Silas said he had plans after school, but I still hoped to see him before he left for his friend's house. I hadn't yet confided to Eva about what had happened with her brother. It was an awkward subject, so I kept the secret to myself.

After three plates of sausage-and-vegetable lasagna, a salad, and two slices of chocolate cake, Eva whisked me to her room. She wanted my opinion on wardrobe selections.

"To wear where?" I asked, holding my hand on my bloated stomach. My loose jeans almost fit.

"You'll see." She flashed a mischievous grin. Her dark eyes narrowed so that her long black lashes seemed even longer.

Eva secured a shiny silver clip high on her head, propping up her hair in an elevated ponytail. Next, she painted on bright red lipstick, making her mouth look dramatic, as if she were about to be photographed for a magazine. She applied more mascara, curled her lashes, and slipped oversized designer sunglasses on top of her head to complete the effect. She wore a slinky, tight gold top with a V-neck and a short, stretchy pale skirt cinched at the waist with two black belts of different widths. Finally, she pulled on patent leather boots with two-inch heels.

"Going out on the town?" I asked.

"Well, the red is a little too much," she said, surveying her lips in the mirror. She removed most of the lipstick with a tissue.

"Where are you going? I thought I was sleeping over. Girls' slumber party."

"Going out on the town. *We're* going out on the town."

"What are you talking about?"

"We're meeting Tom Michaels at Happy's."

"Does your dad know?"

She raised her eyebrows. "Are you kidding? Come on. Now we need to get *you* ready."

"I don't want to be a third wheel," I said, stretching out on the bed, my head propped on one elbow.

"You won't be a third wheel, Lucky. He's bringing a friend."

I sat up straight. "What? Eva, I'm not going."

"Of course you are. It'll be fun."

I jumped up and stared in the mirror. Beside Eva, I looked like the dumpy *Before* picture on one of those makeover shows with my baggy gray sweatshirt, worn jeans, and cosmetic-free face. I had no interest in getting prettied up for anyone but Silas.

"I'll fix you up. It's a major undertaking, but I can do it. I have the tools." Eva waved a hand to emphasize the baskets of blush, mascara, eye shadow, and liner. "You'll look like Miss America when I'm done."

"This boy, Eva. Who is he?"

"Weston Parker."

"Weston? He's a senior. He's so out of my league," I said. My fingers trembled as Eva applied mascara to my lashes. "Please don't make me do this."

"You're nervous. I'll tell you exactly what to do. Ask open-ended questions, ones he can't say yes or no to. Then you nod and look interested, even if you're not. The secret is that boys like to talk about themselves. Let them. He'll think you're the greatest conversationalist in the world and you don't have to say a thing."

"How did you become such an expert?"

"I read lots of women's magazines." She applied a stroke of blush, then pointed to a stack of glossy magazines on her bookshelf.

I breathed slowly, trying to shake the nerves bubbling up inside. Eva finished with the makeup, then said, "Ta-da!" I didn't recognize myself in the mirror. I looked older, at least sixteen. Even seventeen.

"See? You can tell him you're a senior at St. Brigid's."

"I'm not Catholic," I said. "I'm Jewish. Sort of. I'm also in the tenth grade. No way will he think I'm older."

"Yeah, but there's no Jewish school down the road. He probably knows every senior girl at Brickville, but not the sophomores. It's not like you have any classes with him. Plus, you do look older with makeup."

Eva sifted through the hangers in her closet. "No, not this … nope … not quite right … aha! These."

She threw clothes into my arms. Her favorite pair of tight black jeans still fit loosely despite my full belly. She added a periwinkle scoop-neck stretchy shirt and a short, tight black denim jacket with shiny metallic snaps, giving me a faux-curvy figure. Then she handed me large gold hoop earrings and twirled me around.

"Too much. It's too much," I said to the mirror. "I don't look like me. If Mom saw me, she'd spray my face with a hose."

And what would Silas do? What if he saw me out with another boy?

"Your mom won't see you," Eva said. "No worries. You look gorgeous. Now leave your Keds here. Those won't do."

Eva placed blue suede shoes in front of my feet, but they were so big they came off when I walked. Then she pulled out a pair of black leather boots, shoved balled-up knee-highs in the back heels, and said "Voila!" They slipped forward a bit, but I had to admit they looked good. Very grown-up.

We came downstairs and avoided the living room where her parents were watching TV. As she walked out the door, Eva yelled, "Mom, Dad! Lucky and I are taking a walk to the ice cream shop. Back soon."

•   •   •   •   •

High schoolers packed Happy's every Friday night. The wait for a table often took an hour or more.

That night the line snaked through the waiting area to the glass doors. Brickville baseball players and their friends, celebrating a victory over our rival, Edison, filled the booths. Hamburgers, hot dogs, and club sandwiches covered the tables. Frazzled waitresses smiled, rushing between customers and the kitchen, balancing trays of ice cream sundaes, root beer floats, and milkshakes. Happy's was famous for its monster sundaes. Eva and I usually split one, ordering four different ice cream flavors and toppings. Our favorite: chocolate chip, chocolate marshmallow, vanilla, and strawberry ice cream lathered in caramel, hot fudge, marshmallows, and raspberries. But that night, full from dinner and anxious about Tom Michaels and Weston Parker, I didn't want to eat anything.

Eva winked us through the crowd, sweet-talking various boys. Being the elementary school principal's daughter had its benefits, but Eva could probably move to the front of any line, even in a town where she was a perfect stranger. I scanned the restaurant to make sure Silas wasn't around, breathing a sigh of relief when it was clear he wasn't there.

Five minutes after being seated, Tom and Weston walked in. Tom swaggered over first in his blue varsity jacket even though it was warm out. He wore it proudly, the "B" for Brickville embroidered on the top left side next to a baseball. He winked at Eva and grinned, then slid into the booth, turned to Eva and kissed her on the lips. I'd never seen Eva kiss anyone. Tom draped his arm over her shoulders, oozing confidence. His dark hair, curling up at the edges, needed a cut. He looked and acted nothing like the tenth-grade boys.

A minute later, Weston stood next to our table. Butterflies churned in my stomach when I looked at him—but not the good butterflies I experienced around Silas. These were like a side stitch from running too much. He also wore his blue varsity jacket, but he didn't sit down. Instead, he put his hands in his pockets and nervously moved his feet.

Eva said, "Weston, meet my friend Lucky Brilliant. Lucky, that's Weston. Sit."

Weston obediently sat down. I slid over to the wall, giving us plenty of space. He looked at me for a second, gave a half-smile, then picked up the menu. My hands trembled.

"So what do you like here?" he asked in a shaky voice.

"I like the sundaes," I said, "but we had a big dinner, so just a soda."

Weston studied the menu as if expecting to be quizzed on the different flavors of ice cream. My stomach ached. I glanced at his face. He had olive skin and light eyes. His chestnut hair might have been strawberry blonde at one time. He looked nice but I felt funny, as if I shouldn't be sitting there next to him. I would rather have been with Silas.

Laughter and loud talking filled the restaurant. In the booth across from us, four girls from school stared at their dates. Tom noticed them too. He winked at one, a blonde who started giggling, and he smiled at another. Eva elbowed him in the ribs.

We ordered. Tom and Weston talked about the baseball game, then each wolfed down a large sundae *and* chili cheese French fries. I sipped at a soda, my stomach growing more painful with each passing second. I wanted to leave. Halfway through her sundae, Eva caught my eye and kicked me under the table.

"So, Weston. Do you play football?" I realized as soon as I spoke that it was a yes-or-no question. Eva kicked me again.

"Yes," Weston said.

"What position? Shortstop?" I immediately heard my mistake but couldn't take the words back.

Tom burst out laughing. Weston shook his head. "That's baseball," he said.

"Is she slow or something?" Tom asked Eva, whipped cream on the side of his mouth. Then he looked at me. "What grade are you in, anyway? Brilliant? What a joke to have that as a name. You're not so brilliant. False advertising."

Eva poked him again.

"Hey," Tom said, "Didn't your dad die? Like in a car accident?"

I pushed Weston out of the booth. He stood up, clearing the way for me.

"Excuse me," I said, "I've got to go."

Turning away, I dodged the waitresses and pushed past the customers waiting for tables as fast as possible. I heard Eva yell at Tom, "Shut up, you moron!"

I tried to run down the street but Eva's boots kept slipping. Out of breath, stomach hurting, I gasped for air. It was strangely dark. Not a star was visible.

"Lucky! Lucky, wait up!" Eva yelled, her high heels tapping down the sidewalk.

I stopped and waited. Eva caught up and hugged me. "I'm sorry, Lucky. They were jerks. Especially Tom."

I was glad she had followed me.

"Sorry I ruined your night," I said. "Guess I'm simply not ready for any of this. They're too old. I'm only fifteen. You are too, but you seem so much older. I'm such a baby."

"You didn't do anything wrong," she said. "I shouldn't have made you go."

We walked home, my stomach pains fading by the time we reached Eva's house. But my feet throbbed from the boots. We stayed up late, talking and watching old movies, giggling like middle-schoolers before drifting off to sleep.

NINETEEN

Mom lay in bed, saying she needed to rest before dinner, when I heard a knock on the door. A man stood on the stoop holding a clipboard and a manila envelope. *Delivery* was embroidered on his brown shirt.

"Is this 55 Evergreen?" he asked.

I nodded.

"I have a delivery for Chase Brilliant," he said, looking at the clipboard. "Oh. For the family of Chase Brilliant."

I looked past him to the street. He appeared to be alone.

"That's us," I said.

"I'm sorry," he stammered. "I need a signature."

"I'll get my mom," I said, leaving him at the door and heading to her bedroom. She was asleep, her arm draped over her forehead.

I returned to the living room. The delivery man had taken a step inside.

"Do you have any water?" he said. "I might need to sit down a minute."

Stranger-danger popped into my head briefly, but he looked like he genuinely needed help. He was pale, his hands shaking on the clipboard and envelope.

"Sure," I said, pointing to the couch. "Sit there. I'll get you a glass of water."

He had his head between his knees when I returned.

"Here," I said. He drank quickly. "Do you need a doctor? My mom's in the other room. I can have her call someone for you."

As he took a couple of deep breaths, I looked at him closely.

"You look familiar," I said. "Do you have any kids in high school?"

"No, no kids," he said. He looked at the picture of Mom, Dad, and me on the coffee table. "You're the daughter? You have any brothers or sisters?"

"No. It's only me and my mom," I said. "I do recognize you from somewhere. I'm like my dad—I never forget a face."

He looked me straight in the eye.

"The newspaper," I said. "That's it. About a month ago. I remember now. You won the lottery."

He quickly stood up, leaving the envelope on the couch. "I'm fine now. Please sign?"

I took the clipboard and slowly wrote my signature, trying to make it look neat and official.

"That is you, right? I remember because the numbers you played were the same as my dad's. He always played those numbers. Except for that day."

"Thank you," the man said, then left without saying anything else.

I was puzzled. Why would a lottery winner keep his job as a delivery man? What happened to all his money? People were strange; that's what Mr. Kean once told me.

I picked up the envelope. It was addressed to Alice Brilliant. I tossed it on the table and went over to Eva's.

A few hours later, I found a paper that said *Foreclosure* taped to our door.

"Mom! Mom, you've got to get out of bed." I shook her, but she wouldn't budge. She groaned. I shook her again and she finally sat up, rubbing sleep from her eyes.

"What now, Lucky? Can't you let me sleep?"

"This paper was taped to our door," I said. "It says 'Foreclosure' and a bunch of other legal gobbledygook."

Mom pulled off the covers, turned on the light, and sat straight up as if she'd been slapped awake.

"Damn you, Chase," she said. Then she took the manila envelope that had been delivered a week ago and handed it to me. I pulled out the papers and started reading. The heading said Third National Bank and it was addressed *Dear Alice Brilliant.* The first paragraph talked about an advance on future home sales that didn't go through. I couldn't understand most of it, but I figured it was bad. I'd overheard an argument between Mom and Dad a year before about how far behind they were on the mortgage.

Mom threw the foreclosure notice across the room. The papers scattered everywhere.

TWENTY

Mr. Mongelli let me in. He always got up early, even on Saturdays, in his white or blue golf shirt. During the week his elementary school students marked the day by what Mr. Mongelli wore: blue bowtie on Monday, red on Tuesday, yellow on Wednesday, purple on Thursday, and no bowtie on casual Friday, instead a blue Oxford with the top button left open. And always with tan or gray khakis. During the week he wore a blazer, and on days when the Board of Education met, he wore a blazer that matched the color of his pants.

He led me to the kitchen and began eating his usual breakfast of granola, yogurt, and one sliced banana. Though the world changed around him, Mr. Mongelli still saw things as they were. Eva said her mother had gained several dress sizes since they were married but that her father still saw her as a size-two. Whenever Mr. Mongelli bought her clothes, she smiled, kissed him, then quietly returned the item the next day for clothing that actually fit. But Mr. Mongelli was the exact same size as when they met. Eva said that he could still squeeze into his high school baseball uniform. He ran around the track every day after school.

"How are you, Lucky?" he asked between bites of granola and yogurt, putting on the wide-eyed, concerned look that people had started using with me ever since the accident. They were afraid I might break into a pile of broken china right in front of them.

"Fine." I forced a smile even though I was preoccupied with banks and the foreclosure. My stomach growled so much it hurt.

Mrs. Mongelli shuffled into the kitchen. She had on her pink terry-cloth robe. Her hair, mostly gray, stuck up on top. The twins darted past her.

"Stop running in the house!" she yelled.

"Boys," Mr. Mongelli chimed in, but they kept running anyway.

Silas came in next. He smiled at me and poured an overflowing bowl of Lucky Charms. Marshmallows spilled on the table. I returned his smile, the heat rising in my cheeks.

Mr. Mongelli wiped his mouth, took a final sip of coffee, then kissed his wife. "I've got paperwork to do," he said.

I watched Silas eat. What did he think about? Sometimes he closed his eyes and had a calm look on his face, the same expression Mom had when she used to play the piano. I remembered when we would go to the temple and people would close their eyes during silent prayers. They all looked so peaceful, hoping for nice things to happen in the world, their old faces smoothed out. They looked younger. During this quiet time, I almost heard their prayers rising up through the stillness. Then soft guitar music would begin and, one by one, like flowers blooming in the spring, their eyes would pop open.

That's how Silas looked—peaceful. I wondered if in his world of not speaking, he found solace. Our house had been silent for two months, but it was far from peaceful. I didn't want to be home anymore. It was like a morgue. Cold. No food, no laughter, no music. That's why I went to the Mongellis' as often as possible. I was like a refugee, desperate for the noise and warmth that ran wall to wall inside their house.

Would Silas kiss me again? I had liked him for a long time, I now realized. I used to come by even when Eva wasn't home in order to sit with Silas in the living room. Even though Silas said nothing, he comforted me. We played video games. He watched me draw. One day I made a cartoon of him. I put him in a superhero costume with a lightning bolt on the front, a Super Silas who gained powers after the lightning strike. Eva later told me that he pinned the drawing to the bulletin board in his room. But some days Silas seemed far from having super powers. On those days, he would stay in his room. Eva or her mother would explain that he had a migraine or back pain, side effects of the incident.

I loved Eva like a sister but I didn't always understand her moods. Silas, though, understood me. He would take one look and know if I was having a bad day, if I was worried about something or missing Dad. He'd change my mood by writing riddles or jokes like, "What did the hot dog say to the bun?" I'd fall into a fit of laughter and write the punch line: "I'm gonna roll on you." The stupidest joke in the world, but it made me laugh.

Silas pointed to the box of cereal. I ate two bowls before Eva finally made her grand entrance. Beautiful as always, Eva wore a long satin gown that looked like an outfit a bride would wear on her honeymoon. She raised her arms, stretching.

"Hey, Lucky. Eating *Lucky* Charms. Ha ha," she said.

"I've heard that one before."

Silas squeezed my knee under the table. I tried to make my face look natural.

"What's up for today?" Eva asked, sipping water.

I hadn't seen Eva eat a single thing in days. Her arms seemed thinner. Her face, too. Silas passed her the cereal box, but Eva shook her head, shoving it back.

I looked at their kitchen clock; it had different vegetables for each hour.

"Half past the cucumber," I said, laughing.

Silas spit out milk.

"Pig!" Eva said, hitting him on the arm. "Clean it up. You're so gross. Let's go."

I followed Eva into the living room where the twins were watching *SpongeBob*.

Another Saturday morning in Brickville. I wondered where Mom and I would live when the bank took over our house.

TWENTY-ONE

A few days later, on a beautiful April afternoon after school, I was sweeping the Keans' porch when a car rumbled to a stop in front of our house across the street. A young woman with frizzy hair and a tucked-in blouse–J.C. Penney's, probably–got out and stood at the curb. Holding a worn dark briefcase, she studied the house as if she were planning to buy it.

Next door, Mrs. Mongelli pushed her trashcan to the curb. Then she walked over and started talking to the woman. I put down the broom and crossed the street. Mrs. Mongelli saw me and retreated to her house. The woman walked to our front door.

"Can I help you?" I asked, worried that she would post another notice on our door.

She turned and smiled, her red lips overdrawn, clown-like. If she was trying to sell something, she was out of luck. We even turned away Girl Scouts lately.

"Do you live here?"

I nodded.

"Is your mother home?"

"Why? Who are you?"

She handed me an official-looking card. *Brenda Malvern. Middlesex County Department of Social Services.*

"I'm a social worker."

She had kind eyes and, despite the lipstick, a pleasant smile. But there was also something business-like about her, an impatience like she had a lot to do. I sensed her waiting for my reaction.

"Why do you want to talk to my mom?"

"I tried to call first but your phone has been disconnected," she said, not answering my question.

"Wait here," I said, leaving her on the stoop. In Mom's room, the blinds were closed but, surprisingly, the bed appeared empty. It had even been made for the first time in two months. Dad used to say, "What's the point in making a bed? You only use it again." But Mom liked beds made, clothing picked up, the carpets vacuumed often. At least she used to, before.

Now Mom came out of the bathroom dressed in jeans and a polo shirt, her wet hair shiny and brushed. It was the best she'd looked in two months. Maybe her sadness was lifting and things would get better.

Then I remembered the social worker waiting outside.

"Lucky. How was school today?" A simple enough question but one that she hadn't asked in a while.

"Fine. It was fine, Mom," I said. "There's a woman outside who wants to talk to you. A social worker."

I handed Mom her card.

"You should put on lipstick," I said, looking in her closet, finally finding a black blazer. "Here. Dress up a little. You need to look more together."

"Lucky, I showered and made the bed. Got dressed. I'm getting there."

She read the card again.

"I don't understand what this woman wants," she said. "It's probably not about us. Maybe she wants to ask about that new family down the street."

I didn't buy it.

"Well, she's waiting," I said.

In the kitchen I quickly wiped the counter, put away coffee cups, shoved dirty silverware into drawers. Then I saw empty wine bottles lined up next to the wastebasket. I started to pick them up, but it was too late. Brenda Malvern waited in the entry hall. I grabbed two dishtowels and draped them over the bottles.

Mom gave Brenda Malvern a tour of the house. I sat down at the kitchen table and pulled out a notebook and my math textbook, pretending to do homework. I imagined the social worker taking note of everything—the dirty carpet, the scuffed walls, the burned-out light in the hallway. When they came to the kitchen, she smiled at me, then looked around. I was glad that I had straightened things up. She didn't seem to notice the wine bottles beneath the dishtowels.

Someone knocked on the front door and Mom left to answer it. Brenda Malvern turned to me. "So how are you, Lucky? How are things here?"

"Fine. Just fine," I said, biting the inside of my cheek. My voice had cracked, giving myself away. I tried not to look her in the eye. A lump welled up in my throat. I took a deep breath. She kept staring at me, waiting, but I excused myself. In the bathroom, the waterworks began before I closed the door. They didn't stop for five minutes. Over my final sobs, I heard a raised voice.

"What right do you have coming to my house and judging me? You try and be the perfect mom when your husband dies and leaves you nothing!" After two months of sleeping, this new version of my mother surprised me. Brenda Malvern started talking about food stamps and how she could help Mom find a job, what she called "gainful employment." Their voices grew quieter.

So this woman had come to take me away. I had heard of such things. A girl in my class, Julie Hilliard, abused by her young mother, had been placed in foster care. Julie hardly talked anymore. She looked down at the floor all the time as if she were afraid of everyone. Did Brenda Malvern assume Mom abused me, too? Sure, there was little food, and I had to fend for myself most days. But Mom would never hurt me. Not on purpose.

I washed my face and cautiously walked to the kitchen. The two of them were now smiling and drinking tea. What had happened? I went to my room.

A few minutes later Mom came in without knocking. The anger had returned. "Who called the Department of Social Services?"

I remembered Mrs. Mongelli talking to the woman at the curb. Had Mrs. Mongelli called, concerned about my well-being? No, Mrs. Mongelli wouldn't want to get my own mother in trouble. It couldn't have been the Keans. I decided it was a nosy neighbor down the street.

Next to my books on the kitchen table lay several papers left by the social worker, including information about food stamps and employment. Mom picked up the sheet that listed jobs and began circling with a pencil.

That night not even the bats soothed my worries. I didn't have any newspaper dreams foretelling the future. Instead, I had nightmares about being forced out of the house, my hand gripping the front doorknob tightly, refusing to let go. Then the whole house broke apart and I was pulled away, the doorknob still in my hand.

TWENTY-TWO

The next day I took *This Side of Paradise* up the sycamore tree in the backyard. As a child, I spent hours in trees. I would sit on a strong branch with a book and read. Sometimes I'd watch the birds and the clouds floating across the sky.

When was the last time I'd climbed a tree? Reaching for the first branch, I decided I'd climb all the way to the top and never come down again. No one would ever take me away from my home. I was sick of it all—my depressed mother, the silence in the house, the empty pantry and refrigerator, the foreclosure notices. I climbed branch by branch, the book in my jacket pocket.

The more I climbed, the closer I came to the pale blue sky. If I kept going, I might see God. I would ask Him to tell me the reason for taking my father away. I moved to a solid branch and perched high in the tree, wedging my body between two limbs that formed a seat. When I looked down, I was not afraid of falling. What more was there to be scared of?

"Why?" I asked a cardinal that perched on a tiny branch up above. One dark eye stared unblinkingly at me. Determined to never come down again, I opened my book and began reading about Amory Blaine and his lost youth. I was just beginning my life, but I also felt lost. If it was like this at fifteen years old, what did nineteen have in store for me? I was mad. Mad at God. Mad at Dad for dying. Mad at myself. It was my fault that he'd gone out that night for a piece of stupid canvas.

Mom probably didn't even notice that I was gone. I sat there most of the afternoon, hoping she would come looking for me, lodged between leaves and branches, my bottom sore from being poked by the rough surface of the limbs.

The air grew cold. Clouds slid in, dimming the light. Then, nearly dozing off, I heard a voice.

"Lucky, what on earth are you doing in that tree?" Mr. Kean peered up from the base of the sycamore.

"I'm mad."

"Having a tantrum? Aren't you too old for that?"

"Yes. But I'm not coming down. I've been here all day and my mom hasn't even noticed."

"So you've become a tree-sitter, huh?" Mr. Kean rubbed his neck. "Please, Lucky, come down. It's dangerous up there. And it looks like it's going to rain."

His words sounded soft, not booming and sure as usual. Mr. Kean was not melodramatic and he wasn't a worrier. He leaned on the trunk as if testing its sturdiness. He reached up and grabbed the lowest branch. Again and again he looked at me, then turned toward his own house. Was he afraid that Mrs. Kean was watching him? He only made it up one limb before slipping back down.

"Darn," he said, rubbing his ankle.

"Are you hurt, Mr. Kean?" I asked. He shook his foot.

"Old injury. I must have twisted it."

"I'm sorry. Please don't climb up. You'll hurt yourself."

Then I saw Mrs. Kean marching into the yard. She began screaming, her arms waving in the air, grabbing at emptiness.

"Get down! Get down, Emily!" she repeated over and over. Then she knelt on the ground, crumpled into a ball, and sobbed.

Emily? Who was Emily? Not wanting to cause a scene, I moved my foot onto a lower branch, wondering if I should climb down. At that moment lightning flashed across the sky. I grabbed a limb tightly with both hands. Thunder grumbled and a breeze blew the leaves. I looked down at Mr. Kean, who was now comforting his wife. Should I stay put?

Another boom of thunder. Rain began to fall noisily in the branches. The big drops were cold on my arms. The wind grew stronger, the sky darker. Small pebbles of hail pelted my head. More thunder.

I thought about poor Silas spread out on the ground, bleeding from the ears, motionless. I shivered. I was up so high—it was a long way down and the branches were getting wet. What if lightning struck me? What if I couldn't talk anymore?

Rain, hail, wind, thunder.

"Lucky!" Mr. Kean yelled, his arm around his wife. "Get down now!"

"I can't," I yelled above the wind. "It was my fault."

"What was your fault? It's okay you climbed up there. But please come down."

Mom appeared in the yard, rubbing her eyes. Had she been sleeping all day again? Had she finally noticed I was missing? She looked at the Keans and then up at me, shielding her eyes from the rain.

"Lucky? What are you doing up there?"

"It was my fault! Dad died because of me!"

"What are you talking about?" she hollered. "You have to come down! It's dangerous. Remember what happened to Silas?"

"Dad is dead because of me. I should be hit by lightning. I don't deserve to—"

"Lucky, don't talk like that. Come down now."

And then Mom began climbing the tree. I had never seen her do anything that adventurous. Even when the three of us used to hike in the park, she wouldn't climb on the big rocks with Dad and me. Now, though, in the middle of the storm, she pulled her thin body up to the lower limbs as if she climbed trees every day. Her foot slipped and she stopped briefly, adjusting her grip on a branch. She began climbing again.

"If you don't get down here, I'll carry you down!" she yelled.

Mom was trying to save me, but I had to stop her. The only way was to climb down myself. My eyes cloudy with tears, my hair soaked, the thunder still rolling, I moved toward the ground. Slipping off a branch, I banged my knee against the trunk, but I kept going.

"It isn't your fault, Lucky," Mom called out. She crouched on a low limb a few feet above the ground. "Dad was running lots of errands. It didn't happen because he was out getting supplies for you."

Looking at Mom, I was reminded of that T.S. Eliot poem we had read in class last week, "The Love Song of J. Alfred Prufrock," about the pair of ragged claws scuttling against the ocean floor. Mom grabbed at the slick tree but slipped down again.

With Mom's words, and with each pelting of hail, the guilt melted away. But the lightning and thunder picked up again. The rain came in sheets and the wind blew a gale. I froze in place, halfway down the tree. It was too scary and slippery to move.

Then I heard a different voice. A voice I hadn't heard in a long time, familiar but different. And deeper.

Silas.

"Lucky! Wait! Mrs. Brilliant, stay there."

Mom half-jumped, half-fell from the tree. She landed in a heap next to the Keans.

"Mom! Are you okay?" I yelled.

Mr. Kean helped her up. She staggered and brushed herself off.

Then came Silas. Silas, whose life was forever changed by a storm exactly like this one. He climbed with easy agility, branch to branch, reaching me in a few seconds.

"Take my hand," he said, his voice deeper than it had been before the accident. "Don't look down. Follow me."

He descended one limb at a time, reaching up for me and holding my hand as I joined him. We moved that way, slowly and carefully, toward the ground amid the rain and thunder and flashes of lightning.

Mrs. Kean, standing now, hugged me first. Mr. Kean patted Silas on the back, nodded to me, and led his wife back to their house.

Mom stepped forward and hugged me hard. "Lucky, don't ever do that again."

We turned to Silas, who stood sopping wet. We were all soaked. Another blast of thunder sent us running toward the house.

Mom wrapped us both in blankets to soothe our shivering. Then she heated water and made tea. We wrapped our hands around the warm mugs, steam swirling in our faces. Mom ran a hand through my hair, then Silas's. Without saying a word, she left us there at the kitchen table.

"Silas," I said. "You spoke."

"I guess I did."

"What happened?"

"I don't know. I saw you in the tree and my voice suddenly came back."

"It's so good to hear you talk again. Thank you."

"For what?"

"For getting me down."

He cleared his throat. I wondered if it was sore.

He paused, then broke into a grin. "I figured, what are the chances of being struck twice?"

Then he kissed me. And we sat there, shivering out last shivers, quietly drinking our tea.

TWENTY-THREE

The phone rang for the first time since it had been cut off. When I picked up the receiver, Eva's familiar voice yelled, "Finally!"

"Mom must have gotten caught up with the bills," I explained. "But the Steinway is gone. She sold it because we need the money. It's shocking. Anyway, why did you call if you thought our phone wasn't connected?"

Apparently, Eva had been calling every day to see if it worked. She came over that night and I told her about Silas saving my life. She was so happy that Silas could talk again, though she half-kidded that now he would annoy her with his babbling. Then she hugged me. When she let go, she examined my legs and arms as if checking for damage.

"Thank goodness you're fine. You might have been hurt."

"I was just mad. But can you believe it? Silas can talk again."

"Now he won't shut up," Eva said. "Could you please climb back up the tree during the next storm? Another bolt of lightning might shut him up again."

"You don't mean that."

"Of course not. It's great he can talk again. And you should see how excited Mom and Dad are. They called the doctor. Now Mom thinks that it was all in his head. All along they said that there was no physical reason that he couldn't talk. They still don't fully understand lightning-strike injuries."

I changed the subject.

"A social worker showed up."

"I know," Eva said. "Silas overheard my mom say something to my dad about it."

I hesitated. Had Eva's mother been the one to contact the social worker in the first place? Had she betrayed Mom and me?

"I might end up in foster care," I said. "I hope Mom gets it together. That lady is probably coming back to check on us. In a way, it was a good thing, though. Mom's been reading the want ads in Mr. Kean's old papers every day."

Eva sat at the kitchen table. "Have you had any more dreams?"

"No," I said. "I only wish I could go back in time instead of forward."

"Why?"

I stared out the window, trying to find the words in the trees or in the sky. "Because then my dad would be here. I'd beg him not to go out that night, not to buy my damn canvas."

Eva touched my shoulder. "I'm sorry, Lucky. I wish I could change that too."

The phone rang. I looked at the number. It was Aunt Robin.

"I'm coming to Newark," she said. "Psychic convention."

"What? Are you kidding?" I asked her.

"Nope," she said. "There's a convention for every type of business. Lucky, I can't wait to see you."

I once asked Aunt Robin how she got into the psychic hotline business.

"I love talking on the phone and working from home," she said. "I reach out to lonely people. It's kind of like being a therapist."

That wasn't what Mom told me. She said Aunt Robin became a psychic because she was afraid to leave the house, that she was embarrassed about her weight and the cruel comments from people. But I didn't think that was the reason. When Aunt Robin came to Brickville, we always visited the coffee shops and Happy's for ice cream. She always talked to strangers. She'd walk right up and compliment them on a blouse or a necklace, asking for suggestions about the best places to eat in town. Though I did notice that kids stared at her. One time at Happy's, a boy with chocolate and hot fudge smeared on his hands pointed at her and said, "She's fat, Mama!"

Aunt Robin also said she started the psychic hotline to pay her way through community college. She studied stenography and actually had been a court reporter for two months. But the job made her back hurt and strained her eyes. She hated it, quit, and returned to the psychic hotline full-time.

When I heard about the freedom of a home-based business, I began to daydream about that kind of career. I loved to stay in my room and draw for hours at a time. In ten years I'd set up a real drawing table in an office. I pictured other cartoonists working beside me in a high-ceilinged studio with skylights. It might get lonely working at home all day long.

In my fantasy, Eva would twirl into town between gigs in Broadway musicals to tell me about her latest flame. Or she would try modeling, then after being told she wasn't tall enough, she'd switch over to a career as a fashion designer. Lately Eva doodled while I worked on my comic strips. She sketched outlines of trendy shirts and skirts with interesting fabric patterns.

Aunt Robin interrupted my thoughts. She was talking loudly, as if she had to yell all the way from Florida to be heard. "How's your mother?"

I didn't tell her about the social worker, but I did say that Mom seemed better. She had been running around the house like a madwoman, vacuuming, dusting, cleaning the bathroom. There was a lot to do since she hadn't done any housekeeping for two months. She even did the laundry. I wouldn't have to wash my underwear in the sink anymore.

The next day when I got home from school, Aunt Robin's white Chevy van sat in front of our house. Mom called the van an eyesore, wincing whenever she saw it parked at the curb. When Aunt Robin had come for Dad's funeral, Mom made her park two blocks away. Written on both sides of the van, in black script, was Aunt Robin's logo: *Know the Future Anytime / 1-800-PsyChic.* Above the words was an image of a gorgeous woman with big blue eyes and long lashes, her head tilted slightly, her smiling lips red and glossy. Shiny black hair flowed from underneath a multi-colored bandana. She wore big gold hoop earrings.

"Why do you have to drive that van?" Mom always asked her. "Aren't you embarrassed by it?"

"Business has doubled since I added that chick to the van," Aunt Robin explained. "I'm raking in the dough now."

I welcomed Aunt Robin with a hug. She seemed like a different person; since Dad's funeral, she must have lost thirty pounds. I never thought that she and Mom looked anything alike, but I almost saw a resemblance now.

"Lucky, look at you!" she said, holding me at arm's length. "You're so thin! Isn't your mom feeding you?"

"Look who's talking, Miss Skinny Minnie! Have you been on a diet?"

I secretly missed the extra folds in Aunt Robin's back. They always comforted me, big pillows in contrast to Mom's back, which was bony and paper-thin. When I hugged Mom, I feared she might break.

"I joined a gym," Aunt Robin said. "And I'm barely hungry lately."

Her eyes looked funny, kind of wide and shiny. They were the same blue as one of Mom's. I'd never noticed that before.

Mom looked at her with a big smile. "You're in love," she said.

I was shocked. "What? A guy? You said there were only losers out there. Tell me about him."

We sat on the living room couch together as Aunt Robin told the story about meeting Lenny—shockingly, during an attempted robbery of her van. She said Lenny was a big man, six-five and three hundred pounds, but with kind eyes and a great smile. He was walking his dog on the sidewalk when "a punk jumped out from behind the bushes," called Aunt Robin a name, and grabbed her keys. Lenny rushed the would-be thief quickly, slamming him into the van.

"Rule number one: you don't insult pretty women," Lenny said, pinning the guy's face to the van door and twisting his arm behind his back. "Rule number two: stealing is bad. Now apologize to the pretty lady."

By the time the police arrived, the thief was crying and his nose was broken. Lenny had tied his feet and wrists with trash bags. Sure enough, he had apologized to Aunt Robin. At a coffee house next door, she and Lenny rehashed the incident over lattes. They moved in together a week later.

"I have no appetite anymore," Aunt Robin said. "The pounds are melting away."

Mom must have told her about the tree incident.

"What about you, Lucky?" Aunt Robin said. "No more climbing trees during storms."

"Okay," I said, excusing myself to do homework in my room.

An hour later, I slipped into the kitchen for a bottle of water. Mom and Aunt Robin were still talking in the living room. I shouldn't have been listening, but I couldn't help it.

"Chase was as bad as our father," Aunt Robin was saying. "Even worse. Our father had the good sense to leave."

"Dad was a drunk," Mom said.

"I hope this doesn't sour you on men, Alice. I met Lenny. If I can meet a nice guy, there's definitely a man out there for you."

"One crashes his car, leaves me there, and I nearly die," Mom said. "The other one crashes his car and kills himself, leaving me with this mess of a life to fix on my own. Why would I think anything positive about any man ever again? Why should I meet somebody new? So I can get hurt again?"

"They're not all bad. You don't see the signs. I mean, I knew about Chase."

"What are you talking about? You never said anything bad about Chase."

"Forget it," Aunt Robin said. "It's nothing."

"No. Tell me."

What on earth were they talking about? Who left Mom where to die? What bad things about Dad? I shouldn't be listening. I took a step toward my room but stopped. Curiosity got the best of me. I stayed in the kitchen, hidden around the corner.

"Are you sure you want to know?" Aunt Robin asked. "Chase is dead. We should let sleeping dogs lie, Alice."

Mom's voice shook. "I want the truth."

"Okay." There was a pause before Aunt Robin continued. "Remember when you had that party here years ago? That first party?"

"Sure. After Lucky was born. A house-warming party. We invited all the neighbors."

"You were in your room nursing Lucky. It was the end of the night. Most everyone had gone home. I was out in the kitchen cleaning up."

"Go on."

"I saw Chase and your neighbor."

"Who? Maria? Maria Mongelli?"

"Yes. Mrs. Mongelli. The one who used to be the famous model. Dark hair, tall, very pretty."

"So she was here. They were … what? Talking?"

"Kissing. Out in the backyard. On the other side of the workshop."

I didn't want to hear anymore.

"It was Maria? Are you sure? Did you have your glasses on?"

"Alice, I wear glasses for reading. I can see things that are far away."

Mom's voice became fierce. "I don't believe it. That was early on. We were happy. We were so happy. I gave him a daughter."

"It wasn't just a kiss. They vanished into the workshop. I stood there rinsing wine glasses, putting dishes away, one eye watching. Twenty minutes. They were in there twenty minutes."

Mom lowered her voice as the anger crept in.

"Why didn't you tell me? Why are you telling me now, when he's dead and I can't do anything about it?"

"You'd had a baby," Aunt Robin said. "I didn't have the heart to. It could have been a one-time thing. Men feel abandoned after a child is born. They want attention. I was hoping it was that one time."

"I've been living next door to that woman all these years. My daughter is best friends with her daughter. I can't accept it."

"You need to move on," Aunt Robin said. I pictured her holding Mom's hands. "Knowing this will help you. It's easier to forget about someone you don't miss."

No way, I thought. Not Dad. Aunt Robin was wrong. About all of it. She must have seen another person in the backyard that night. It was probably Mr. Mongelli out there with his wife. Or maybe it was Dad, and he took her into the workshop to show her the dollhouse, the one that was still out there, unfinished.

Then I remembered that the dollhouse didn't exist then.

TWENTY-FOUR

I ran to the workshop. It was precisely the way Dad had left it.

The dollhouse stared at me. It was an eyesore, like an abandoned house overgrown with weeds. When I was five, Mom and Dad had taken me to visit friends in upstate New York. One afternoon Dad and I swam in one of the Finger Lakes, then hiked a few trails. We found a house that someone had begun to build and then abandoned. Of course, I insisted we explore it. The drywall was hung but not painted. There was a roof, but the doorknobs and appliances hadn't been installed. In the July heat with all its windows closed, the house grew steamy inside. Suddenly I heard buzzing—a swarm of bees had fled their hives in one of the walls. Dad grabbed my hand and we ran as fast as we could. Three bees stung me on the way out.

Looking at the unfinished dollhouse, I felt like I had been stung all over again. Dad had promised it would be finished years ago when I still played with dolls. Every time I asked him about the house, he shrugged, smiled, and said, "Next year, Lucky." He would describe his elaborate plans, drawing sketches of the blue roof tiles and the molding he was going to order. The appliances would look like the fancy Thermador ovens in kitchen and house magazines. A tray ceiling would adorn the living room. Dad had even found an artist who would make replica figurines of us all, even Monty. He was so wrapped up in his plans that I forgave him the endless delays.

"When I'm a famous actor and we live in Beverly Hills, our house will be like this. Only a little bigger, of course," he said. Then he would talk about the time he was in a real movie. He had read about a casting call for extras in a movie about the Mafia that was shooting in Atlantic City. It was R-rated, but he and Mom took me anyway on the night that it opened at the Brickville theater. I remember the movie was full of Italian actors who reminded me of Eva's family, with dark hair and brown eyes. During one scene on the crowded boardwalk, Dad pointed to the screen and whispered, "Look close. That's me in the white shirt."

When the movie ended, he asked, "So what did you think of your old man?"

"Well, it was kind of hard to see you," I said. "I recognized your hair and your walk, but I couldn't see your face. I thought you had a speaking part."

"I did," he said. "They must have cut it. They do that in the editing room. Even the stars have their dialogue cut."

He seemed quiet and a little sad.

"You're famous," I said, guilty that I had taken away his smile.

"Yeah. At least I can add it to my résumé. It's a real film credit. The phone should start ringing off the hook any day now. I'm sure the agents in Hollywood will be contacting me."

It was difficult to tell if he was being serious. We were walking away from the theater. Mom put her arm around him and said, "You did stand out from the other extras. The camera loved you."

"Really?" Dad smiled at her as if starving for a compliment. He was acting like Mom did when she was unsure if an outfit looked good before a big night out.

"Of course," she said.

Dad leaned in and kissed her.

But the phone calls never came. At night Dad paced the living room, stopping in front of the phone, picking it up to make sure it worked. Then he would bang down the receiver. After a month he continued acting in the community theater, but he told the story of his film debut to anyone who would listen. The story changed, growing larger and longer with time: "I had lunch with Pacino. He gave me his personal number. He might hook me up with his agent."

People seemed captivated when Dad gave these accounts. He could deliver an entire story with hand gestures, his fingers and palms sluicing the air. Those hands made him unbeatable at charades. He had long fingers, long but not too lean, with neatly trimmed nails. His hands were clean and smooth; they weren't like the gnarled, calloused hands of construction workers or carpenters, people who didn't have office jobs. In the small town of Brickville, Dad had become a star. No one else we knew had appeared as an extra in a big movie before. At parties, men and women gathered around to hear him recount his experience.

As I remembered all of this, I had a new thought: What if these women wanted more from Dad? If the affair with Eva's mother had actually happened, did that mean there had been others? Last month Eva had read an article to me from *Cosmopolitan* about how men were inclined to be with more than one woman. How if they cheated once, they cheated again.

In front of the dollhouse sat the miniature door. Dad had never attached it. I turned the wood over in my hands. Then I threw it as hard as possible. It banged off the back wall of the workshop, the little brass doorknob breaking off. "You cheated on Mom!" I yelled, the loss and anger welling up in a wave. Then I pushed the entire dollhouse off the worktable. It crashed to the floor, wood and plastic scattering.

My own house was falling apart, bit by bit. Pieces inside me were crumbling too. What else didn't I know?

TWENTY-FIVE

The next day I walked to school alone. Eva was sick with a cold and Silas was at a doctor's appointment. I wouldn't have been good company anyway.

Near Main Street I spotted the mystery man again, the one wearing the Mets baseball cap. I quickened my pace, determined to catch up with him. The strange thought followed me with each step: Could this man be Dad? Was he alive? He was in the middle of a crowd of men and women walking to the train station. I kept my eyes on the Mets cap bobbing in the distance. A whistle blew, the squealing of brakes signaling the train's arrival. On the platform I spotted the man stepping onto the train. Instead of going to school, I ran up the ramp and, without a ticket, boarded the train to New York.

I raced from engine to caboose looking for the orange and blue of the Mets cap. No luck. On my way back up the aisle, a conductor appeared. He started to collect tickets. I walked through two more cars but I was trapped. My heart pounded as he approached. I looked left and right as if I were lost. What should I do?

"Ticket?" he asked, dark circles beneath his eyes.

"I can't find it," I said, checking my pockets.

His skin sagged like one of those sad-looking dogs. He shook his head.

"You alone?"

"Yeah," I said. "I have an appointment at an art school in the city. I can't find my ticket. It was right here." I pointed to my upper pocket.

He put his hand on the brim of his New Jersey Transit hat. He looked like the kind of man who didn't like to wait. In the front pocket of my jeans I found a ten-dollar bill.

"I can buy another one if I have to," I said. "But then I wouldn't have any money for lunch." I made the saddest face I could muster.

The conductor stared at me for a moment. Then he moved on to the next passenger. I took a deep breath. It felt as if I'd been underwater for too long. Finding an empty seat, I stared out the window watching old buildings and dying trees pass by. I'd ridden the train before, but never alone. Mom and Dad often took me to the half-price Broadway tickets booth in Times Square on weekends. We'd seen forty-two Broadway and twelve off-Broadway shows. That didn't include the countless plays, including Dad's, at the Brickville Community Theater.

An announcement blared over the intercom for Metropark, then Elizabeth. Tired, I closed my eyes, the rhythm of the train lulling me to sleep. Suddenly I saw the back of the man in the baseball cap sitting in front of me. He turned around— it was Dad! He smiled at me. Then flames burst out, his face turning to smoke.

I snapped awake. Just a dream. At least this one wouldn't come true.

Then an announcement: "Next stop, Newark." The train slowed to a halt. Passengers exited, entered, and the train started again.

Finally, we arrived at Penn Station. As I walked off the train, I looked at the throng of people on the platform. How could I ever find the man in such a mob? I pushed forward, wondering where I had found the courage, or foolishness, to ride the train by myself into New York City. It probably wasn't the safest place for a clueless tenth-grader with poor navigational skills to be on a school day. Eva could find her way through the city; she was smart that way. But the thought of being in the city alone frightened me. The tall buildings, busy crosswalks, fast-moving cabs. The noise and the scents seemed foreign to me. I breathed deeply and put one foot in front of the other.

And then, in the middle of the sea of heads, I spotted the Mets cap. I followed it up a set of steps, my shoulders bumping into the herd of people. We moved onto the street and into an onslaught of beeping horns, blaring sirens, and rumbling trucks. As suddenly as it had appeared, the Mets cap vanished into the crowd again.

I felt small and lost. Scared. I let myself be carried along by the swarm of pedestrians. A few split off to the left, crossing the street. Others hustled and bustled down the sidewalk. Yellow taxis flew by. Homeless people stood or sat, begging for money. I tried not to look at them, but their sadness tugged like a hook that had caught me around the neck. Would Mom and I become homeless too? True, the foreclosure notices had disappeared and the phone worked again.

But the money from the sale of the piano wouldn't go far. How would we survive? Would we end up with our backs propped against a building in New York City, our bottoms chafing against the cold, dirty concrete, our hands out begging for money?

The Mets cap was nowhere in sight. The thin air bulged with the scent of rotten trash and urine. Claustrophobic and dizzy among the skyscrapers, I walked forward. The volume of people began tapering off. I realized I was turned around. Completely lost.

I roamed unfamiliar streets. Graffiti covered the sides of buildings. Boys walked by in jeans that hung below their hips, boxers exposed. A group of teenagers on a corner whistled. Other people spoke in foreign, rapid tongues. Loud car radios blared hip-hop tunes. Old men sat on steps, drinking from crumpled bags, staring out at the streets. Staring at nothing.

"Hey girlie!" somebody called. I quickened my pace, aware of footsteps following me. I started to run, pumping my legs even faster than when the bees had chased me. I remembered a story that Eva told me about a girl from the high school who snuck into a dance club in the city. Three teenagers assaulted her in an alley outside the club, and she ended up in a hospital for the next six months. Trying to outrun the memory of that story, I found myself in the middle of a street. A yellow taxi nearly ran me down, screeching to a halt in the nick of time as I waved my hands and yelled, "Stop!"

"I'm off-duty," the Jamaican-accented driver said, pointing to the unlit sign on top of his taxi.

"Please," I begged. "Please take me to Penn Station."

He stared at me, then nodded. "Get in, little missy."

"Penn Station. I want to go home. Take me to Penn Station," I said, imagining Dorothy clicking her red shoes together.

"First time here?" he asked.

"No. I just got lost."

He weaved, honked, and jammed his breaks for several blocks.

"Ten dollars," he said, pulling in front of Penn Station.

"Mister, how much does a ticket cost to Brickville?" I asked, holding out the ten-dollar bill, my hand shaking.

"Keep it, my dear. Consider it a favor. I have a daughter your age. It's your lucky day. And bring your mother or father next time. You shouldn't be wandering into certain neighborhoods here alone, even during daylight."

"Thanks."

Back at Penn Station, I read a map on the wall, bought a ticket to Brickville, and left the city. My disappointment kept me alert. On the train I stayed awake this time, wondering about the man in the Mets cap, how he'd morphed into my father while I slept on the train. I'd skipped a day of school chasing a dream. What was happening to me?

●　　　●　　　●　　　●　　　●

Walking home from the station, my mind raced. If Mom asked why I wasn't in school, I would say early dismissal. So I was becoming a liar, too. But Mom wasn't there. Where was she? Without a car, she never left the house. I waited until three when Eva would be home.

Next door, Eva answered my knocking and put her finger to her lips. We silently walked through the house, down the hallway past the living room where Mom sat on the couch. I started to talk, but Eva pulled me into her room before Mom saw me. Silas sat on Eva's bed. Something was wrong. They both looked at me, a little scared, I thought.

"You're not going to believe what happened," she said. "Do you want to tell her, Silas?"

Silas chose silence.

"Your mom came over about an hour ago," Eva said. "She asked my mom if she had called the social worker."

I wasn't surprised. After all, I'd had that same thought.

"What did your mom say?"

"No, of course," Eva said. "She wouldn't do that."

I had to defend Mom. "It's been rough on Mom, Eva. You can't blame her for trying to find out who ratted on us."

Eva turned to Silas. He stared at his feet.

"That's not all," Eva said. "She asked my mother if she had an affair with your father."

Having overheard Aunt Robin and Mom, I could guess where this was headed. But I didn't know the answer.

"She asked my mother if it was a one-time deal or a weekly occurrence. She wanted to understand how she found the time for an affair with four kids and all her shopping."

I bit my lip. "And what did your mother say?"

Eva's chin trembled. Silas decided to answer.

"She apologized. She said it happened only once. That she felt flattered by your dad, that she had been upset about getting older and gaining weight. She liked the attention your dad gave her."

So there it was: Dad had fooled around with my best friend's mother. I wanted to run home and hide under my blankets with Monty. How could he have betrayed us? How could Mrs. Mongelli have done this?

Eva continued. "She said that your mom should forget about the past and start focusing on you. She said she didn't call the social worker but that maybe she should have. She told her about how she'd been giving you meals, watching out for you the past two months. And that's when you came over. Lucky, I'm sorry. So sorry."

I felt angry and embarrassed about my family. Disgusted. Shamed. Humiliated. Tears began. Silas reached for my hand, but I grabbed it away. I stomped down the hallway to the back door. I didn't care if Mom or Mrs. Mongelli saw me. No one followed.

Later, Mom didn't say anything about her confrontation with Mrs. Mongelli, and I put it out of my mind as much as possible. In fact, I accompanied the Mongellis to Eva's big dance recital the next day. We didn't talk about the affair. Eva looked beautiful on stage twirling and leaping in a ballet solo. She later performed in a group jazz ensemble. Afterwards, the Mongellis took me to Tony's Restaurant for a white-tablecloth dinner. Mrs. Mongelli was as kind to me as she always was. I tried to convince myself that nothing had happened between her and Dad. But I knew it had.

TWENTY-SIX

Skinny, bald, and pale, Mr. Harrington looked like he'd been teaching since the French Revolution. His monotone voice droned on and on. To make matters worse, the classroom was stifling. The air conditioner was broken; hot air poured through the windows. Holding my eyes open became a real challenge.

Outside, honeysuckles clung to fences and walls, open like little petals of sun. I imagined their sweet smell. In the courtyard bright flowers framed a new memorial bench for the assistant principal, Mr. Benson, who died suddenly last year during an assembly in the auditorium. He fell right off the stage while the mayor was talking about the benefits of helping others in our community. Ironically, no one rose to help Mr. Benson, not at first. We were all stunned at how suddenly tragedy could appear in our lives. Mrs. Mongelli took the lead in raising money to buy the bench in Mr. Benson's honor.

I remembered how Mom had always been active in school. She never missed an assembly. And last fall she filled the position of PTA vice president. But after Dad died, she resigned. She hadn't set foot on the school grounds since.

As Mr. Harrington spoke, I opened and closed my hand, trying to stay awake. Then I drew a cartoon version of myself as a super student. In the first scene, I plowed through the dull white wall of the classroom. In the second, I sat outside on Mr. Benson's memorial bench, leaning toward the honeysuckle. Then I leaped into the air and hovered over Main Street, above Mr. Geller's art studio, the coffee shop, the train station, and the funeral home. I flew above New York City and the New Jersey swampland. In the last panel, I sailed with the seagulls over the waves at Atlantic City, looking down at Dad's face, a ripple beneath the water. His hand reached out to mine.

A bony finger tapped my slumped shoulder. I had fallen asleep. Startled, I lifted my head, knocking my pencil to the floor.

"Miss Brilliant, am I keeping you awake?" Mr. Harrington asked, his breath full of garlic. He folded his arms across his skinny chest. The patches on his blazer jutted out as if his elbows were knives.

"Sorry," I mumbled. "It's stuffy in here."

"Perhaps it would be cooler in the principal's office."

"No, I'm wide awake now. Sorry for dozing off."

I slid my drawing beneath the thick textbook and tried to listen as Mr. Harrington resumed his lecture. But the sun and yellow flowers outside called me away. The image of Dad's face returned.

· · · · ·

After school I walked to Mr. Geller's studio. A different foster kid greeted me when I entered through the door at the top of the stairs above Happy's.

"Hey," he said, looking up from his painting. His white T-shirt was covered in splotches of red, black, and yellow.

"That's pretty good," I said, studying his canvas. "Looks like a nightmare."

"That's exactly what it is. I'm even calling it *Nightmare.*"

A figure with wings hid in the corner.

"A bat?" I asked.

"Yeah. Mr. Geller thinks it represents the dark side."

"Dark side of what? The moon?" I thought about *Lord of the Flies,* the book we were reading in English.

"The moon. The subconscious. Yin and yang. A doppelganger." He smiled at me. "You choose."

He wiped paint smears on his jeans, then extended his hand. "Mick Saint."

"Mike?"

"No, Mick. My parents couldn't decide between Mike and Nick. And they were Mick Jagger fans, so …"

He looked like an artistic version of Silas, with light eyes and dark hair, only his hair hung to his shoulders.

"I'm Lucky."

"And you think 'Mick' is odd?"

"It's actually Lucy. Long story."

"Okay. Lucky it is."

"You one of Mr. Geller's temporaries?"

He looked back at *Nightmare*. "Is that what they're calling foster kids these days?"

I shrugged.

"For a while," he said.

I looked around the open room. "Where did Emanuel go?"

"He took off. He's in the city sleeping on his friend's floor. Got a job as a waiter. He's painting in the mornings."

"Do you have parents?"

"I did." Mick dipped his brush into black paint and started another bat in the lower corner.

I didn't ask any more questions—his painting said it all. Did he lose both his parents? At the same time? To have lost one was awful enough. I tried to imagine not having Mom. Even though she hadn't been much of a mother lately, at least she still existed. And I loved her. What would it be like to be an orphan? I thought about that tsunami in Indonesia where hundreds of children became instant orphans after the water swallowed their parents.

Shivering, I rubbed my arms. The studio was the opposite of Mr. Harrington's classroom. Mr. Geller kept it cold to preserve the paintings. I'd read that museums did that so the paint wouldn't fade in the heat.

"Grab my sweater." Mick must have noticed. "I put it in the closet."

I found an old, oversized wool sweater on a hanger. As I was putting it on, I noticed a stack of magazines on the floor. I picked up the top one, *Art World Today*, and recognized the young face staring back at me. It was Baxter Geller under the headline "The Next Picasso." His eyes were different, the way a person looks before unwrapping a present, as if the box might contain anything. Possibility. It was the same look in Dad's eyes when he talked about making it big in the movies.

"Find it?" Mick asked.

I shut the closet door, sat on a stool, and watched Mick work for a few minutes. Something was tugging at me. It was like a splinter in the tip of my finger that needed to be pulled out. What if the social worker came back and took me to a foster home? Would I end up like Emanuel and Mick, moving from home to home, the property of the state of New Jersey? Or would I be shipped off to live with Aunt Robin in her tiny apartment, listening to her give psychic predictions to callers at all hours of the day and night? I couldn't bear to leave Mom, or Eva, or

Mr. Kean. And what about Monty? Who would take both a fifteen-year-old girl and an energetic Italian Greyhound?

Mr. Geller entered quietly through the front door. He held a takeout coffee cup. "Afternoon, Lucky. Have you made any progress? If you want to enter that show, we need to get moving."

I slid the wooden stool over to my own canvas, took out the paint, and pushed away my questions, focusing on my work. With each stroke on the canvas, I fell into the moment, into the paint, immersing myself in the color. The worries about my future slowly slipped away.

TWENTY-SEVEN

An amazing thing happened when I got home. I heard it the moment I pushed open the door. Thinking I must have walked into the wrong house, I hesitated in the hallway. Familiar music on the stereo: Chopin. The scent of muffins wafted through the kitchen and into the hallway. The smell of sugar and blueberries. Pancakes, syrup, eggs.

"Mom? What's this? Breakfast for dinner?" She stood by the stove in a denim apron, flipping a pancake. Her hair looked clean, brushed smooth and newly trimmed. Yellow roses sprung from a crystal vase in the center of the table.

"I got a job. We're celebrating."

"A job? Where?"

She slid two pancakes onto a plate. "The Stop Mart, down the street."

"Stop Mart? Are you a cashier?"

"Assistant manager," she said. "It doesn't pay much but it's a job. If I work full-time I get health insurance, which we do need. And I can move up."

"That's great, Mom," I said, hugging her. She smelled of vanilla and soap, the way she used to. But she was too skinny. I worried that if she lost any more weight, she'd turn into a younger, female version of bony Mr. Harrington.

"I start tomorrow. Let's eat up and enjoy."

Except for the few dishes in the sink from dinner, the kitchen appeared spotless. Pine-Sol filled the air. The oak cabinets glistened, newly polished with lemon oil. The tables and windows shined so much, I saw my reflection. In the bathroom, laundered plush towels hung from the racks. Even the brass fixtures gleamed.

I slept well that night, the sound of the bats lulling me to sleep. I only woke up once when my hand went numb. Beside the bed stood an outline of a figure. Dad? His hand reached for mine. I rubbed my eyes—*another dream*, I murmured, then turned over and fell back to sleep. But when my alarm buzzed in the morning, my hand still tingled with warmth.

Life was on the upswing in May with Mom receiving a steady paycheck. The pantry was filled with jars of spaghetti sauce, bottles of juice, and boxes of noodles, cookies, and granola bars. Students called and wanted piano lessons again, so Mom checked into leasing a cheap piano to supplement her income.

Sure, problems did sprout from time to time. One day Mom finished her morning shift at Stop Mart and came home to discover the kitchen ceiling leaking onto the linoleum. She slipped on the puddle and twisted her ankle, the same one she'd hurt while climbing the tree.

When I got home from school, a large plastic bowl sat in the middle of the floor. The drip-drip-drip sound clued me in to the problem. An area of the white ceiling was dark and bubbled, a sagging circle ready to pop. Mom limped around the house saying, "Why now? What else?" She raised her arms toward the ceiling as if God hid in that moist, protruding pocket. The bowl was the same one in which Mom mixed cookie batter. I had a brief image of Dad sticking two fingers in the bowl. A week before he died, Mom had baked his favorite chocolate-and-butterscotch cookies. He snuck up to the bowl and stole batter, lifting a dollop into his mouth, then into Mom's.

"Wait until the cookies are baked, for Pete's sake," she mock-scolded him.

"We should just eat the batter," Dad said, reaching down for another ball of sweetness.

She hit his hand lightly. "Always in such a rush, diving in before things are ready."

I joined the party, eating until my belly ached, splatters of dough freckling the island.

Now I stared at the water bleeding into that bowl. Reality, leaking into life again.

"Did you call a plumber, Mom?"

"Of course I did," she said. "He should be here any minute. Not that I can pay him, though. Things were finally coming together. Why? Why?"

"It'll work out," I said, patting her shoulder. "It's probably nothing major."

A few minutes later a man with a toolbox waited at our door.

"Plumbing Pros," he said. "I'm Danny. Hear you've got a leak."

He wore a tan work shirt with the script *Plumbing Pros* beneath an embroidered silver faucet. He had thick arms. I imagined him unblocking pipes all day long.

Mom showed him to the kitchen and explained what had happened. Danny listened, then asked a few questions. What room was above the leak? Had we been having any problems with water pressure? Each word he spoke was laced with a funny accent—Irish, I later learned. I had to keep from laughing. His blonde hair curled up at the ends.

Danny brought in a ladder and began working. I noticed Mom acted differently around him. She quickly shifted from being annoyed to girly, almost giggly, which was odd because she wasn't a giggly kind of woman. I thought about the popular tenth-grade girls. Mom's voice sped up and seemed an octave higher. She laughed at what he said even when it wasn't very funny.

After he'd been working a while, Mom returned to the kitchen with her hair down. She ran her fingers through the back section, then twirled the ends. I'd never seen her playing with her hair before. Ever.

Danny started at the bubble, cutting all the way to the light fixture that hung over the kitchen table. Soon he was explaining how water travels and how to find the source of a leak.

"There it is," he said in his Irish brogue, dusty bits of drywall snowing in the kitchen.

"Can you repair it?" Mom asked, fear creeping into her voice.

"Sure. But you'll have to get a contractor to replace the drywall. We don't do that."

"Oh," Mom said. "Does it cost a lot?"

He stepped down and wiped his hands on his jeans.

"I'm a widow," she blurted out. "My husband died and I'm trying to get back on my feet financially. Do you have a payment plan? I don't mind a hole in the ceiling. I just don't want the hole to leak."

Danny smiled, his face lighting up. He looked like a young boy.

While he finished his work, Mom sat in Dad's old chair. She stared ahead as if trying to pull numbers out of nowhere. Why was she telling a stranger our business? That wasn't like her.

I started my homework. Even with the door closed, I heard a strange sound. I couldn't make out what Danny was saying, but I could hear Mom laughing more than she had in a long time. More than ever before.

I didn't understand why it bothered me. Instead of being happy for Mom, I missed Dad terribly.

The next day, after school and working at the Keans' house, I discovered that the plumbing had not only been repaired, the holes in the ceiling were patched. Mom was talking on the phone. She wore a pretty silk blue blouse, blush, and eye shadow. But the biggest change wasn't the ceiling or her clothes or her make-up. It was the smile plastered on her face. Who was this woman?

"It's called heterochromia," she said into the phone. "You are so observant. I do have one blue eye and one green … your favorite colors? Both of them? How funny … Tomorrow? Sure, eight o'clock. I love Indian food."

Mom loved Indian food? This was news to me. When she hung up, I crossed my arms and tapped my foot.

"Indian food? You hate Indian food, Mom. Who was that?"

"Lucky, you're home. I'm going out. Look." She pointed at the ceiling.

"I see. Fixed. Was it expensive?"

"Danny is so nice. He said not to worry about it. He'll hold the bill for a while."

"Mom, are you going on a date?"

"I told you. I'm going out, Lucky. No big deal."

"Dad just died. Aren't you in mourning?"

"Lucky, I'm tired of mourning. Perhaps it's time to move on."

I thought of Mom resting in bed for two months. The empty bottles of wine. The lack of food, how the shelves in the pantry and refrigerator had been empty for weeks. Seeing Mom happy was a nice change, I had to admit. Of course I didn't want her back in bed, but I wasn't sure if I wanted her *this* happy either.

Mom scribbled in *8:00 dinner with Danny* for the next day on the wall calendar. When I looked at her loopy writing, the room turned cold. I had been so distracted by Danny and the plumbing problem that I had neglected to notice the date: May 10. It had been three months since Dad died. I wondered if another dream would come soon.

TWENTY-EIGHT

That night I had another newspaper nightmare. The headline: *School Activity Bus Crash Kills Driver, Student.* The high school track team bus, on the way to a meet in Edison, apparently slid off the road during a torrential rainstorm, killing the driver, Mr. Petrick, and the star hurdler, Jeremy Jackson. Other students sustained various injuries, from broken bones to a collapsed lung, lacerations, and bruises.

A photo of the mangled bus flashed below the headline. Beside that, Jeremy Jackson's senior yearbook photo stared at me in black and while. He had curly light brown hair, dark eyes, and a square jaw. He was one of the boys Eva once had a crush on. Jeremy had won all kinds of championships; his tall, shiny trophies lined the high school display case. Eva told me that his father worked for the sanitation department and that his mother had run off with the postman ten years earlier, never to be heard from again. Jeremy and his father had been thrilled when he earned a full scholarship to Jersey State. Eva had the scoop on every boy in town, especially the athletes.

I saw another photo in the dream—Mr. Petrick's son Derrick, a junior like Silas. His hands covered his face, but I recognized him anyway. Derrick had the same black hair and sharp chin as his younger brother, Sherman, who was a sophomore. A quiet kid, Sherman often came out with witty, surprising one-liners, so clever that last year I had to run out of the biology classroom in the middle of a frog dissection, nearly peeing my pants from laughing so hard.

I had met Mr. Petrick once because he'd been one of Dad's clients. I had gone with Dad to show Mr. Petrick and his girlfriend a townhouse. After losing his wife to cancer, Mr. Petrick finally met a nice Ukrainian woman at his church. I remembered how his face glowed as Dad showed him around the townhouse. Mr. Petrick hugged Katriana outside when they decided it was the right home for them.

I woke up at three in the morning too scared to return to sleep. It was my second newspaper nightmare following Dad's death. Would it come true the way the bank robbery had? I got out of bed and paced in the darkness. Above me in the attic, I heard the faint sounds of the bats. After the eerie silence of the dream, the noise was comforting.

I turned on my desk lamp and looked at R. Crumb's drawings taped above my desk. I wished his Truckin' cartoon gave me an answer. "What would you do, Crumb?" I asked out loud. The cartoon character's fingers pointed toward Dad's workshop. I shook my head and climbed back into bed.

Eight o'clock came quickly. I woke up fuzzy-headed, glad it was Saturday. Then I remembered that Saturdays were track meet days in the spring, so I raced to Dad's workshop, ignoring the mess of the broken dollhouse on the floor. On his work table I found what I was looking for—Dad's bright green address book, the same color as his Upward Mobility blazer. Sure enough, I found Mr. Petrick's phone number inside.

It was early but I dialed the number, figuring out what I would say. I imagined Mr. Petrick, Katriana, Derrick, and Sherman eating breakfast together in their cozy townhouse on Grove Street.

He answered on the second ring.

"Mr. Petrick, it's Lucky Brilliant."

"Lucky, how are you? What a surprise. Do you want to talk to Sherman?"

"No. Actually, I want to talk with you. This is going to sound strange but I have a question. Are you driving the track team to Edison today?"

"No. The meet was postponed. I'm going to drive them there Monday."

I twisted the phone cord tight around my fingers.

"Don't. Just don't. Please. Call in sick. Switch routes. Don't drive them there."

"Lucky, what's the matter?"

"Something bad is going to happen. I know it."

"I don't understand how, Lucky. I'm sorry about your father. How are you doing? How's your mother?"

I wasn't getting anywhere with Mr. Petrick, so I asked him to put Sherman on the line.

"Hi," Sherman said. "What's up?"

"I'm not crazy," I blurted out. "You have to help me here. A terrible thing is going to happen to your dad if he drives the track bus Monday. If I'm right, and I definitely am, you'll never forgive yourself."

Sherman asked what I'd been sniffing.

"Nothing, Sherman. Please tell him to stay home. Or at least not to drive the track team."

I hung up. I didn't care that the Petricks thought I was out of my mind. Maybe I was losing it. But if I saved two lives and countless injuries, it didn't matter what anyone thought.

A knock on the front door startled me. I thought it might be Danny here to check our plumbing. Worse, it might be the social worker to check on us. Instead, it was a burly man with frizzy hair tied in a ponytail and a long, straggly beard that reached his bulky chest. He handed me a card smeared with dirt—a picture of a raccoon along with the words *Ron Oz / Oz Rescue Service*.

"Your mother called. She said you have a bat problem."

"We have a few bats," I said, "but they're not bothering anyone."

"Miss, I'm only responding to the call," he said, looking behind me.

The scent of soap and lemon reached me before Mom did—the new Mom, dressed and ready for the day.

"Thank God you're here," she said. "I should have called sooner. They've been here a while. I'm trying to tie up loose ends. Follow me."

She walked down the hall toward the attic pull. I thought of the constant scratching, the high-pitched lullaby that comforted me at night. Sure, Mom seemed more like her old self, and soon piano music might even fill the house again, but a valley of loss opened in me. I remembered carrying that sickly bat in Dad's gloves and setting him free. I liked to imagine that weak bat had recovered and sneaked back in the house, joining the colony in the attic.

I followed the bushy-bearded man up the attic stairs. The back of his shirt read *I Brake for Squirrels*. I felt safe behind his wide blue jeans and thick tan boots. Mr. Oz seemed like the kind of man who would protect people. He pointed to a high corner where beams jutted out, near a vent with slats that let in a stream of faded light.

"You shouldn't breathe this stuff in," he said, somehow aware that I was behind him. "You might get a disease."

"Like what?"

"Nasty stuff. From the guano. It can hurt your eyes. And other things."

Small, dark brown bats clung to the ceiling. Soon they would exit the vent to find food. There were dozens. I stepped backwards toward the stairs, holding my hands near my face, ready to protect myself at a moment's notice.

"You won't hurt them, will you?"

"Nah. I'll make it so they can fly out but can't get in again."

"Where will they go?" I thought about the homeless people in New York and the foreclosure sign tacked on our front door. I thought about Mr. Geller's foster kids, who drifted in for a few days and disappeared. Where had they all gone?

"They'll find a new home," Mr. Oz said. "A barn or a house. A cave."

After one more look at the colony, I slowly descended the steps, wondering if I'd ever be able to sleep again in a house filled with silence, darkness, and prophetic nightmares.

TWENTY-NINE

A cloud filled my head at school on Monday. My mind spilled over with anxiety-ridden thoughts. The weekend had seemed endless. Eva's family had been away visiting relatives. Mom had gone to dinner with Danny. I spent two days trying to pass the time drawing, reading, and watching TV, anything to avoid thinking about the track meet at Edison. All through geometry, Western Civilization, and English, the front-page photo of the mangled bus crashed through every voice and thought.

During lunch, I absentmindedly bit into a strawberry jelly sandwich. Eva snapped her fingers and said, "Wake up, sleepyhead."

Jolted by her voice, I nearly dropped the sandwich.

"What's going on in that spacey head of yours? You've hardly said a word today."

Around the cafeteria everyone laughed, talked, and scarfed down their lunches. Brat Nelson threw part of his sandwich at another table, showing the geeks how daring he could be. Pieces landed on the head of a chubby girl who sat with two girls in the band. When Brat saw me staring, he quickly stopped throwing food, then sank low in his seat until only his mop of messy hair was visible. A kid beside him punched his arm. The steady chatter and laughter of the cafeteria was a comfort, kind of like the subtle bat noises in the middle of the night. I missed the bats.

"I had another nightmare about a newspaper story, Eva. That's the second one. I hope it doesn't come true."

Eva sat there, her brown eyes wide and her arms crossed. She looked exactly like Mom did when she didn't believe me.

"You still think I'm crazy?"

"Not at all," Eva said, closing her eyes and placing one finger on each temple. "I am Eva the psychic. I can read your mind."

"Fine," I said. "Make fun of me. The other thing happened. The bank robbery and Mr. Johnson dying. I told you it was going to happen and it did."

Eva sipped her diet soda. "Plenty of people have strong intuition. My mother guesses about stuff."

She looked around to make sure nobody was listening.

"Like last night," she whispered. "I snuck out to see Derrick Petrick. I did the fake lump-under-the-covers routine and then climbed out the window. But when I got home, Mom was waiting on the front porch. She hadn't even checked my room. The covers were still pulled over the stuffed animals on the bed. How did she know? It's like that. Intuition."

A chill ran up my neck at the coincidence—Derrick, the boy in the photo with his face down, grief-stricken at the news about the fate of his father in the bus crash. I didn't want to tell Eva the details of my nightmare. Not yet.

"Derrick, huh? A mere junior?"

"Yeah. At first I didn't like him. He's not a stud looks-wise, but the more I talk to him ... he's funny. I don't mind his long nose. I really like hanging out with him. And he's the best kisser."

At that moment, an image of kissing Silas popped in my head. "That's great. I'm happy for you. Now do you want to hear about the dream?"

She set her mozzarella stick down and sipped her soda.

"A bus crash. The track team."

"Sounds bad," Eva said. "You don't look so good. Are you okay?"

"I will be if Mr. Petrick doesn't drive the team today."

"Mr. Petrick?"

"I called him Saturday. He probably thinks I'm off my rocker. But I met him once. Dad sold him his townhouse. I found his number and told him not to drive to the track meet, that something awful would occur if he did. I'm hoping he'll switch routes with another driver. Or call in sick."

"Did he listen?"

"Maybe."

"Thank goodness I'm not on the track team," Eva said. "I'm taking the bus to the dance team competition in North Brunswick today. It didn't happen in North Brunswick, did it?"

"No, you're fine."

Eva wiped her mouth. She balled up her cheese, mostly uneaten, in a napkin. She flashed a wide smile across the room. "Don't look now. Donnie Cook is staring at us."

"Boys? You're thinking about boys now? And I thought you liked Derrick."

"I do, but I like to keep my options open," she said. "I'm only fifteen."

"Going on thirty." I shook my head and finished my jelly sandwich, savoring the chunks of sweet strawberries, food we never had in our house when Dad was alive because of his allergies. A piece of strawberry dripped on the table. I scooped it into my mouth with two fingers.

"Strawberry?" Eva asked.

"I could never have it before. Want some?"

"No, I'm full." Eva scanned the room, her gaze pausing at the two tables where the jocks ate.

Something hit the back of my head. I pulled a chunk of banana from my hair.

"Babies," Eva said. "All of them. Babies. I can't wait until college."

With that she rolled her eyes, stood up, and stomped out of the cafeteria.

•   •   •   •   •

Mom was pacing the living room when I got home. I put my backpack on the kitchen table and grabbed a cookie.

"You seem antsy," I told her.

"I'm fine."

"What's wrong? Plumbing leaking again?" It was our inside joke lately, that if Mom looked worried, it must be a leaky pipe.

"Just distracted. Before you came home, a woman showed up at the door."

"Who was it?"

"I don't know. There was a car parked across the street when I got home from Stop Mart. A little red sports car. I saw a person inside. A while later the car was still there."

I followed Mom into the living room. She looked out the window toward the street.

"Ten minutes later the doorbell rang. I asked her what she needed. She didn't say anything. She looked like she was going to cry. Then she turned and walked away."

"Was she selling something?" I asked.

"No. She wasn't carrying anything," Mom replied.

"What did she look like?"

"Long hair in a ponytail. And a beige overcoat, too heavy for spring."

"Did you recognize her?" I asked.

Mom shook her head. She took a deep breath and changed the subject.

"Anyway. How was school?"

"Okay. I was a little distracted. I had a bad dream last night. It's sort of been hanging over me all day."

I wanted to tell Mom about all my dreams, but they would only worry her. Since she had her new job—and, I had to admit, since she'd gone to dinner with Danny—she was acting normal again. I didn't want to spoil that.

"At least the bats are gone," she said. "No more nightmares about being bitten in the neck and getting rabies."

"I didn't have dreams like that."

"I did," she said, trying to lighten the mood.

"I don't know. I sort of miss them." My stomach began hurting.

In the kitchen, Mom started dinner. I took Monty for a short walk, then he curled up on the couch with me to watch TV. As I flipped through the stations, a Breaking News banner stopped me. The image was shot from an overhead helicopter. It showed a yellow bus on its side surrounded by emergency vehicles off a two-lane road. I was scared to turn up the volume. If Mr. Petrick had listened to me, then why this bus crash? The words that scrolled beneath the photo said everything: *Brickville School Bus Crashes in North Brunswick. 2 Dead, Dozens Injured.*

The light in the room swirled in a dizzy circle of dots. I tried to steady my shaking hands on Monty's back. Eva's dance competition was in North Brunswick.

THIRTY

Machines flashed and beeped beside Eva's bed on the third floor of St. Peter's Hospital. Her right leg was wrapped in a cast, her left leg stitched from ankle to knee. I couldn't believe it—her dancer legs. She was sleeping, most likely knocked out from painkillers that dripped through the IV.

I thought about a conversation we had a week ago. We were watching a news report focusing on young soldiers returning from Iraq with severe injuries–a few without legs, others who had lost arms. One poor guy had a chunk of bone blown from his head and now had a metal plate in its place.

Eva had turned to me. "Which body part would be the worst to lose?"

"My right hand," I said without hesitation. The mere idea of not being able to draw sent shivers through my body. I remembered clutching a pencil tightly to fend off such dark thoughts.

"My legs. Both of them," Eva said, the easy smile gone from her face. I tried to imagine Eva off her feet. It wasn't only the dancing. She was like a spinning top, always twirling into or out of a room. Even while sitting, she pointed her toes and flexed her calves.

I held her hand as she lay in the hospital bed. The room smelled like bleach and sickness. It was a hospital, after all. Through the window to the hallway, I saw the Mongellis talking with Mom. Silas slumped over in a chair in the waiting area. I stopped to see him. He tried to smile when I rubbed his back.

The nurse told me that Eva was in the clear, but I had a hard time believing it when I looked at her pale face. Once in a while she would moan, and I'd move closer to hear what she was saying. But it was babble, nonsensical mumbling. Doctors' names were announced over a loudspeaker. It reminded me of school, how only a few hours earlier Principal Glass had made his afternoon announcements and I had returned home, jittery and restless. After seeing the news report, I ran to Mom in tears and begged her to let me go to the hospital. She still didn't have a car, so Mr. Kean drove us. Sensing the urgency in my voice, he floored the gas pedal instead of driving his usual slow speed of fifty miles an hour on the highway.

In the waiting room we joined Eva's parents and Silas. They wore brave faces for the other relatives and friends. Mr. and Mrs. Mongelli periodically left the room and returned with updates on Eva's surgery. I noticed that Mom looked the other way when Mrs. Mongelli spoke. After a while I sat in a chair next to Silas. He squeezed my hand. I knew he wasn't saying anything by choice this time. There wasn't anything to say.

I listened to the adults talk about the accident. They spoke of the two seniors who had died and mentioned those who had been injured. It became clear what had happened. Mr. Petrick had indeed listened to me and switched bus routes with another driver. But when a third driver called in sick, Mr. Petrick's route changed again. He had to drive not only the dance team but also the track team to North Brunswick. If he hadn't asked for a different route, would Eva have been on the other bus that hadn't crashed? Would there have been a different outcome if I had simply said nothing? Had I, in fact, caused the crash?

And, unlike in the dream, Jeremy Jackson did not die. After the bus flipped over, Jeremy climbed out a broken window with only a scratch on his chin and a bruise on his arm. Smelling smoke, he climbed back into the bus and carried Eva to safety. Added to his track star status—the new title of *hero*.

Mr. Petrick, though alive, was badly injured and recovering down the hall. On the way to see Eva again, I passed his room and nodded to his sons and Katriana. Her face was puffy, mascara smeared beneath both eyes, her hair a loose, frizzy mop.

There was a sour taste in my throat. Poor Eva. Her right leg had broken in two places. In the coming days, doctors would perform another surgery to insert a metal rod in the leg. Would she ever dance again?

A nurse adjusted Eva's IV drip and wrote notes on her chart.

"Time to go, honey," she said, not looking at me. "She needs her rest."

"She'll be okay, won't she?"

The nurse looked like an older version of Mom but with brown eyes. She stopped writing for a moment and nodded. "She'll recover, but I'm afraid her dancing days might be over. For a while, anyway."

I left the room quickly. Silas and the Mongellis looked up, but I walked down the hall, passing the nurses' station and the vending machines, unable to stop the tears.

THIRTY-ONE

Mr. Kean dropped us at home. It was after ten o'clock, but I couldn't slow my heart down. Sleeping would be out of the question. Clenching my fists, then wiggling my fingers, I tried to imagine what life would be like if I lost the ability to draw. If I couldn't use my right hand, I could learn to draw with my left. If both hands failed, then there were my feet. I could train my toes to hold a brush or pencil.

But Eva wouldn't dance again. Surely it took two working legs to dance. The nurse's voice echoed in my head. Could she have been wrong? After all, she wasn't a doctor. And Eva was tough. Perhaps she'd surprise them all and would soon be standing on tiptoes, twirling circles around the stage, flying through the air. She'd been so excited about the dance competition, the upcoming play, and her spring recital. Tears rolled down my face all over again.

Though it was late, I walked back to Mr. Kean's house. He sat in the dark on his porch, rocking back and forth. A sitcom blared loudly from inside. He stared straight ahead, as if in a trance.

"Hi, Mr. Kean. Mind if I sit with you?"

The air was warm and thick. All traces of the rain were gone. A man on a bicycle pedaled down the street guided only by a thin beam of light.

"Lucky," Mr. Kean said, "you don't have to ask."

I rocked quietly for a moment, comforted by the slow back-and-forth motion and the steady song of the wooden floorboards creaking. Exhausted, I thought I might fall asleep right there. But I had to ask him a question.

"Mr. Kean, do you believe in God?"

"The ten million dollar question," he said, staring into his yard. "Well, I do believe in a higher presence. Why?"

"I don't think I believe in God anymore."

"You used to, but now you don't?" He kept rocking, his voice even, as if we were talking about the weather.

"Right. And I used to believe that there was something after death. Now I think when you're gone, you're gone. There's nothing else. Like a cup that's filled with soda. When it spills out, nothing is left but the cup."

Mr. Kean thought a moment. "Wine frequently stains the cup, or a few drops make a deep red stain on the tablecloth."

I shook my head. "But the cup is still empty."

"Didn't you go to temple at one time?"

"Years ago. The temple pre-school. I thought about God as a warm, loving being. Like how a grandfather should be, but up in the sky looming over the world. He would protect my family and me."

"So what changed?" he asked, holding his unlit pipe between his thumb and index finger.

"No God would take away a father like mine. No God would hurt my best friend and destroy her future as a dancer. No God would take away those two innocent teenagers."

"Well, let me ask you a question, Lucky. If we all lived forever and never suffered loss, then would we appreciate our time here? If one day you couldn't draw, wouldn't you draw constantly?"

"Why can't we live forever? Why not live without sadness and loss?"

"I shouldn't have given you those books. Maybe you weren't ready."

I rocked a bit more, looking into the dark sky, searching for stars. They seemed hidden or gone.

"What do you think, Mr. Kean? You're much older than me."

"Thanks for the reminder."

"I mean, you must have lost family and friends by now. I'm only fifteen, and I've lost my father and almost my best friend. More people if you count Dad's parents. But I never met them, so they don't count."

Mr. Kean put down his pipe and stopped rocking. I imagined he was counting in his head as if each life were a pearl on a necklace.

"Yes, Lucky, I have lost many people. My mother and father. Both in-laws. My twin brother."

He stared straight ahead into the dark toward the tree stump in his front yard. "I'm sorry," I said.

"And others. Too many to count. I used to get angry, Lucky. I used to yell at God. Raise my arms and curse him. I remember standing at my brother's grave when no one else was there. I kicked the dirt, found a rock, and threw it at the headstone. It bounced off and hit me in the leg. Anger is a boomerang, Lucky. If you throw it out to the world, it's what you get back. It burns you up from the inside. It changes how you interact with everyone. Trust me, I was no fun to be around when I was like that. And I was like that for years."

"You? You're so calm. I can't imagine you as an angry man."

"Imagine a world where no one believes in anything—whatever you want to call it. A higher source. A spirit in the sky. Hope. Imagine a world without a deity to pray to. A world where no one is listening to all those thoughts."

"There's no sense to anything," I said. "No point. We talk to an empty room, an empty church or temple. No one is listening but our own selves. We make stuff up to believe in so we can make it through the day. Maybe there's only air and space and death."

"My girl," Mr. Kean said. "You are becoming a fatalist at fifteen. You're too young to be thinking this way. I wasn't like that until eighteen. No more philosophy books for you. Return them at once."

I couldn't tell if he was kidding or not.

"I'm almost sixteen, Mr. Kean. Anyway, it's not just the philosophy books. It's even in the poetry I've read. What about 'The Love Song of J. Alfred Prufrock'? Talk about no hope: 'Till human voices wake us, and we drown.' Or something like that."

Mr. Kean rocked again. "My suggestion for the next few months, Miss Almost-Sixteen, is comic strips. Happy, funny comic strips. At least until Eva gets better."

I laughed. "Dad loved funny things. *Monty Python. Saturday Night Live. Mad TV.* Both his parents died early."

"He had the right idea. Humor might be the key to leading a happy and positive life."

"Yeah, but look where that got him." I managed a forced smile. I didn't know if Mr. Kean could see me in the darkness.

"Lucky, I know you miss your father. But to appreciate life, to appreciate the life around us, there has to be death."

"But he was only thirty-nine. He only lived half a life."

"People often pack an entire life into a short time. Like Eva Perón. Marilyn Monroe. John Kennedy. Heck, most of the Kennedys. Their stars burn brighter, but they burn out faster. You've heard that, right?"

"Yeah." Birdsong trilled from the side of the house, a strange sound at night.

"Mr. Kean, what do you think happens after people die?"

"Perhaps a part of them stays with us," he said. "In birdsong. In stars, in flowers, in blades of grass. In clouds and rain. Flakes of snow. Have you ever felt a shiver up your spine when you're alone in a room? I've had that happen. I always think it's someone who is no longer alive letting me know that they are with us."

"Every so often, I hear footsteps," I admitted. "Like someone's behind me. But when I look, no one's there."

We rocked in silence for a minute.

"Feel any better?" he asked.

"Yes. Thanks."

When I got up to leave, he grabbed my hand.

"You remind me so much of someone, Lucky. That spark you have in those green eyes."

"Who?"

"One of those people that I loved."

Mr. Kean always seemed on the verge of saying something important. Perhaps he'd tell me one day. It didn't seem my place to ask.

He let go of my hand. I stopped the rocking chair with my foot. But as I went down the steps, I heard the creaking again, as if a person were sitting there rocking beside Mr. Kean. It made me shiver.

THIRTY-TWO

After working for Mr. Kean the next day, I visited Eva at the hospital. She lay in her bed groggy and incoherent. Mrs. Mongelli said she slept most of the time. Another surgery was scheduled for Monday. I tried to send positive vibes her way. I thought about praying, but since I didn't believe in God anymore, I only held Eva's heavy hand, squeezing it. I wondered if she even realized I was there.

Back home, I decided to take a long walk. I grabbed ten dollars and a bottle of water, then slipped into my new Keds. I figured I could break them in and at the same time sift through the thoughts racing through my head. I passed Main Street and kept going, walking through town, ending up in Heritage Park. I liked the park for its pond filled with ducks, the acres of trees, the abundant hills, the basketball courts, the covered barbecue areas with wooden picnic tables, and the gazebos scattered here and there. High on one hill sat an old brick hospital. I heard that polio patients were once sent there decades ago, isolated from the healthy population, to recover or die. Sickness and death followed me everywhere, it seemed.

Resting on a bench near the pond, I watched the ducks. A white one glided along, skimming the surface, holding up its neck proudly. A line of five black-and-white baby ducks followed. Where was the daddy duck? Was it up to the mother duck to raise these young ones alone? I made a mental note to look it up when I got home.

At the base of the hill was a family of four—a mother, a father, and two girls—sitting on a blanket, a straw-woven picnic basket in front of them along with paper plates and containers of food. A small tan dog stuck his snout near the food and wagged his tail. Family. My family would never look like that one. What if Danny

Boy moved in or married Mom? Could we be a family? He was a stranger. How could he ever be anything close to what Dad had been? I shook the thought from my mind like a duck shaking water from its feathers.

I sipped the remaining drops from my bottle and threw it in a trash can. Bees floated around the top. I slowly moved away, realizing the bees only wanted the rotting waste. They reminded me of the hike Dad and I had taken on our trip to New York years ago, how the bees had chased me through the field and stung me. Had that been a warning? I had tried to change the future, to prevent people from dying. But two girls had died anyway. If I hadn't called Mr. Petrick to warn him, would he and Jeremy Jackson be the ones who died?

What would have happened if I had chosen to do nothing?

Then there was poor Eva. She shouldn't have been hurt. Had I kept my mouth shut and ignored the dream, maybe she would still have her dancing legs. I needed to talk to an expert about the future—Aunt Robin.

I was wrong about the bees that were circling the trashcan. One departed from the others and followed me. It landed on my arm. In an instant the anger inside me flew into the palm of my hand, the same palm that the fortune-teller years earlier had read and declared, "You're a lucky girl!" In one swift swat, I flattened the bee against my skin. It stung me at the same time, but I was so filled with pain inside that I didn't care.

I walked through the park and back to Main Street, stopping for a turkey-and-cheese sandwich at a lunch shop near the train station. A girl from class waved from the sidewalk. Others walked by: an older couple holding hands; a young girl with a ponytail skipping next to her mother; a middle-aged man walking a Labrador, its tail banging against the sandwich store window.

After eating, I stopped in front of the funeral home. Cars, including a long black limousine, filled the parking lot. Should I go inside? Against my better judgment, I entered the crowded funeral and grabbed one of two open seats in the back of the room. Everyone wore black dresses, suits, and skirts except for a few teenagers in golf shirts and tan pants. I had on my pink cotton top, blue shorts, and Keds.

Organ music filled the room. Large displays of colorful flowers decorated both sides of the open coffin. In the front row a woman, tall even while sitting, lowered her head. Her shoulders shook. I couldn't see her face, but her blonde hair looked silky and natural like the hair of a younger woman's. Beside her an older woman with wiry gray hair draped her arm around the blonde woman's shoulder, holding her up as if she were in danger of falling over.

A woman in front of me whispered, "Such a tragedy. And so young!"

"Only thirty-five," her friend responded. "So handsome. And a doctor. Ironic, isn't it? An oncologist getting cancer. His poor girls."

I couldn't see the family in front, but as if on cue, a little girl in a velvet lilac dress jumped up and wandered down the middle aisle to the back of the room. She stopped at my row, looked up with pale blue eyes, then sat down in the empty seat next to me. Her hair was a thick mass of blonde ringlets. She handed me a program and tilted her head as if she had a question.

The organist stopped playing. A minister at the lectern began talking about the deceased man. He quoted passages from the New Testament. I blocked out the words and turned to the girl who looked about five years old. She stuck out her shiny black shoes to show them to me. Then she touched the patch of yellow and green flowers attached at her velvet waist.

"Pretty," I whispered. "I wish I had a dress like that."

A scream pierced the air. Another girl, whom I assumed was her sister, suddenly yelled, "Where's Daddy?"

"My daddy's sleeping in the box," the girl next to me said matter-of-factly.

I opened the program. On the second page was a photo of her father. His blonde hair and wide smile mirrored the girl next to me.

"Will my daddy get up soon?" she asked me. "I miss him. He used to read *Goodnight Moon* and *The Foot Book* to us every night."

"Your mommy can read to you instead."

"No, Mommy cries all the time. And she doesn't change her voice like Daddy does."

"My daddy used to do that," I said. "He could talk with accents. He was an actor."

"Is your daddy sleeping in a box, too?"

At that moment, her mother flew down the aisle crying inconsolably. She stopped when she saw her daughter, then she looked at me and ran off toward the ladies room.

"Yes," I told the girl. "And he was young and handsome. Like your daddy."

"Who reads you stories now?"

"I read to myself. And I have a neighbor, Mr. Kean, who gives me books to read. You must have someone else who can read to you. A grandfather or an uncle or a neighbor."

"I'll ask Mommy. When she stops crying."

The girl walked back up front to sit with her family. When the minister finished and the mourners started to leave, I approached the coffin. The deceased doctor looked plastic, like the man I'd seen at the other funeral. Stiff and lifeless.

On the way home I thought that how, years from now, those poor girls probably wouldn't even remember their father. At least I had memories.

• • •

The next day Mom attended her widow's grief group. They had been meeting weekly in the basement of the Methodist church.

"Lucky Brilliant!" she shouted as soon as she came home. Her anger was unusual. Since meeting Danny, she'd been in a good mood, using a singsong voice and dancing around the living room. She even rented a piano and started playing. She was considering teaching again, too.

What could I have possibly done to annoy her?

"Mom?"

She crossed her arms and narrowed her eyes. "Why on earth have you been going to funerals? Funerals of people you don't know?"

"Who told you that?"

Dad always told me that if I didn't want to answer a question, I should ask one.

"Two people at my grief group. But that doesn't matter. I showed everyone your picture, and they said they recognized you. From their husbands' funerals."

"Why are you showing pictures of me to strangers?"

"We were talking about our families. But that's beside the point. Don't change the subject."

"Did I break a law? Why do I have to prove that I had a connection to the dead? I wasn't carded at the door or anything."

"Lucky, it's nice to be there for other people's grief. To show your respect for the dead. But these are strangers. Why on earth are you crashing their funerals?"

"True, I didn't know them when they were alive, but I know death. The dead are all the same."

"I don't understand," Mom said, unfolding her arms. She sat on the couch and patted the cushion next to her with a freshly manicured hand. I had never seen her nails painted with anything but clear polish before. Was she wearing pink?

I sat beside her.

"Why would a normal fifteen-year-old girl be hanging out at funerals? You should be at the mall. At movies with friends."

"Mom, you haven't noticed, but I'm not a normal girl lately. It hasn't been normal for months. You lost your husband and I lost my father. And my best friend is in the hospital."

She raised her hand and touched the scar on her chin.

"I know, Lucky. Of course I know. But funerals of strangers?"

"It's like I'm closer to Dad. Closer to my sadness. All those grieving people—they understand. A whole room of people feeling what I feel. At school I'm with giggling, silly, nerdy teenagers. I can't relate to them. They don't get it. And I can't go to the mall and have fun. That's not normal anymore. Funerals seem more normal."

She squeezed my hand and looked out the window. A red finch flitted by. Yellow roses bloomed. I remembered the flowers on the little girl's velvet dress. How was she doing?

"Mom, do you want me to stop going?"

"No. But you must tell me what you're up to, what you're thinking. I'll go with you if you want me to."

"Thanks," I said, taking her hand. "Pink nails, huh? Got a date tonight?"

"Danny's taking me to a movie." Her cheeks flushed as pink as the polish. For the first time in a long while, I felt genuinely happy for Mom. Then I noticed her left hand—her wedding band was missing. When had she taken that off?

Nothing would ever be the same again.

THIRTY-THREE

Eva returned home at the end of May hobbling around on crutches. Mrs. Mongelli drove us to school every morning. Mom said I shouldn't be catching rides, but Eva clearly needed me. I helped her out of the car, handed her the crutches, and carried her backpack. We had almost every class together, so I became Eva's assistant. When we weren't together, another friend, Marlee, filled in.

Eva wasn't the same girl. She seemed like a horse with a broken spirit. No longer able to twirl in and out of classrooms, she hobbled along, her smile gone, the brightness in her eyes faded. Despite the fact that boys paid even more attention to her, offering to carry her books or her lunch tray, she didn't seem to care. I hadn't heard her mention even one boy's name since the accident. She spent long sessions in the guidance counselor's office. Eventually, they seemed to help.

I felt guilty. One day she brought up my dream.

"Lucky, I thought you said the bus was going to crash in Edison. It crashed in North Brunswick. And you said it was the track team only, not the dance team."

I burst into tears. "It's my fault. All my fault."

Eva handed me a tissue. "It's not. When I got on the bus and Mr. Petrick was there, I should have turned around and left. You said he'd be driving. I felt it too— a queasy sense that I was in danger, that the bus wasn't safe."

"I ruined everything," I said. "I shouldn't have done a thing. I shouldn't have called Mr. Petrick. Then he'd have driven the other bus."

"But the other driver called in sick. It was going to happen either way."

"If I had left it alone, maybe the other driver wouldn't have called in sick. I changed the future. And because I did, you were hurt."

"It wasn't your fault," she said. "I do miss dancing. But since I don't have rehearsals, I have more time now. I've been doing a lot of sketching. I have pages and pages of drawings for a clothing line, for kids our age. I showed them to my grandma. She's friends with a designer who wants to turn my drawings into real clothes that I can actually wear."

Eva smiled for the first time since the accident.

"I'm glad, Eva. I know how satisfying it is to draw. And when your designs are turned into actual clothes, I'll be your model. Well, not a model exactly, but I'll try them on, give you my honest opinion."

A familiar grin appeared, the kind that used to flash across her face when a boy entered the equation. "Guess who's been calling me?"

"One of your many admirers? Let's see—some Princeton guy? How about Tobey Maguire?"

"You're too funny. No, Derrick Petrick. He's so different. He doesn't care about popularity or sports. He cares what I think about things. I can seem shallow, but no boy ever asked me about anything important before. He wants to hear my opinions. What I like. It's hard to explain."

"I get it. He likes you for what's inside, not just the surface stuff."

I suddenly realized that this was how it was with Silas, too. While Eva had been in the hospital, he'd been hanging out with me most days after school. Sometimes we drew together. Sometimes we watched television or talked. And sometimes we looked into each other's eyes and kissed. When we did, it seemed like time stopped. Nothing else existed but the two of us.

"Yeah. Like that," Eva said. "Lately, I've been feeling terrible about the two girls who died. I want to do something for them."

"Like the bench memorial for the assistant principal? That kind of thing?"

"Maybe. I could sell my designer clothes. I have tons. Not just the ones in the closet. There are boxes stored in the basement, too. And I could write to famous people, ask them for donations, even sign things. A George Clooney autographed motorcycle helmet. Bruce Springsteen-signed CDs. I could organize an eBay auction, get television coverage. Grandpa has all those New York connections. The old stars."

"It's a great idea, Eva. I'll help. But what would you do with the money?"

"Create a scholarship fund in the girls' names for high school students to study dance."

Eva reached down and tried to scratch beneath her cast.

"Need help?"

"Would you mind? It's so itchy."

The cast was no longer white. It was covered with a rainbow of magic marker signatures along with hearts, good wishes, and song lyrics.

"Looks like the entire high school signed it," I said.

"Mostly tenth-graders. And teachers. Thank God I'll have it off for most of the summer. I'd hate to sit by the Brickville pool or in the sand at Belmar in the heat with this sucker on the whole time."

Summer. It seemed so far away. Would I spend my days with Silas? Would I have another dream? And if I did, would I try to change the future again? Or let things be?

THIRTY-FOUR

I was tired and agitated after spending the evening at Eva's labeling her Hermès scarves, designer dresses, and fancy shoes and hats. I had written descriptions of donations from stars that filled the floor and window seat in her room. Three weeks earlier, her grandmother had sent a press release to friends at the *New York Times* and *Los Angeles Times*. As a result, boxes from famous singers, musicians, and movie stars arrived daily at the Mongellis' front door. We stored the overflow of goods in my room.

No doubt existed about the future of the scholarships that would be established in the names of the two deceased students. The scholarships would be well-funded. As for Eva, I'd never seen such a drastic change in a person. She had transformed into a selfless do-gooder. Now she cared more about others than about the contents of her own closet.

I crawled into bed. Monty slept beneath the covers, whining and growling as if he were caught in a nightmare. I was afraid to have another dream that would foretell the future. If I hadn't been so tired, I might have stayed up all night. But after photographing hats, guitars, couture, shoes, and jewelry, I was zonked.

•　　•　　•　　•　　•

Desperate Man Kills Realtor for Lottery Ticket. Two photos appeared beneath the headline—Dad and the murderer. I recognized the murderer immediately. It was the deliveryman.

I thought I was screaming in my sleep, but it was Monty yelping. I must have kicked him out of bed during the nightmare.

•　　　•　　　•　　　•　　　•

In the morning I tried to act normal. I brushed my teeth, dressed, ate breakfast, and walked Monty. The day was anything but normal, though. Besides the dream swirling in my head, it was the last week of school. Everyone acted excited. Even the teachers joked as they handed out grade reports and directed parties. We signed yearbooks and filled our stomachs with pepperoni pizza, cupcakes, and warm soda.

After school, Eva had an interview at a local radio station to promote the eBay auction, so I walked home alone. I needed to clear my head. Passing the funeral home, I noticed a full lot. I hesitated. Fighting the urge to go in, I remembered the conversation with Mom. Full of sadness, I kept walking. It was always this way at the end of the school year. Though glad to be finished with the homework and the boring classes, I was sad about not seeing my friends over the summer. I was also nervous about junior year, which meant SATs and college tours. Planning for the future. Juniors and seniors always seemed so worldly, with their smart clothes and makeup. On top of that, I had grown two inches this year, but I was now only a hair over five feet. I still looked like a freshman.

And then there was the dream. Would they ever stop? Was I nutty?

I looked forward to an afternoon of distraction working at the Keans'. Soon I would be old enough to get a real job, one at the mall or the bookstore in town.

"Last week of school?" Mr. Kean asked. He rocked in his usual spot on the porch, a newspaper on his lap.

"Yup. Summer's nearly here."

He quickly folded the paper and stuck it beneath the seat cover of the rocking chair. It seemed odd. Was he hiding it from me?

"What's new in the news, Mr. Kean? Anything juicy?"

He was staring at my house. I turned and saw a car parked in the street. It was black with a long antenna on top.

"Do you know who's at my house, Mr. Kean?"

"I have an idea," he said. Then he patted the chair next to his, removing the newspaper from under the seat cover before I sat down. "You should read this."

I grabbed the paper and scanned it quickly: *Desperate Man Kills Realtor for Lottery Ticket*. The photo of Dad and the murderer/deliveryman. Same as my dream. I stopped rocking. Mr. Kean placed a hand on my shoulder.

"I'm sorry," he said.

"It's still my fault. It changes nothing."

"What do you mean, Lucky? How is it your fault?" The crease between his eyes grew deeper.

"Dad died because of me."

"I'm confused. Right here it says someone murdered your father. How is that your fault?"

I shook my head, the guilt rising in my chest like a large bubble. A sharp pain jabbed my side as if I'd suddenly gotten a stitch from running.

"He went out that night to buy me something for school. A canvas for a stupid project. If he hadn't gone out, that man wouldn't have killed him. See? It's my fault."

"The what-if game. You'll drive yourself bonkers playing that, Lucky. I used to. Your father chose to go out. That man chose to hurt him. If anyone is to blame, it's this man," he said, pointing at the photo. "You didn't push your father off the road. This man did."

His name was Wilbur Puckett. He was from Perth Amboy, a few towns over. After running Dad off the road, he waited a few days to claim his prize for the Jersey Cash 5 winning ticket—$250,000. At the time he said he was going to use the money to pay for medical care for his sick wife. But then, weeks later, she died.

Eventually, Wilbur Puckett, overcome with grief and guilt, turned himself in.

I couldn't read on. But the dull ache in my side began to lift. I had carried my own guilt for so long, it had become part of me. Some of that guilt belonged to Wilbur Puckett.

"It says he was depressed," Mr. Kean said. "His wife was dying. He was taking medication that might have made him violent."

I looked at Dad's photo. It was the same photo that he sent to agents, the same photo in the community theater display case. Dad would always be this age. I don't know why I had that thought, but I did. I traced his face with my index finger—the strong outline of his jaw, the dark and wavy hair like mine. I smoothed down my own hair, which had grown past my shoulders. It was alive, touchable. But I would never touch Dad's hair again, or have staring contests with him, or laugh with him watching our favorite TV shows. We would never read comics together on Sunday mornings.

The family pattern had repeated for a third generation. Another Brilliant patriarch dead before forty. Dad would never be Mr. Kean's age. He wouldn't rock beside me or beside his grandchildren on a porch, reading stories and giving advice. One day I would be older than Dad was in this photo. How strange.

He was gone. Gone.

And who was the man beside him in the paper? Did he look like a murderer? I remembered Wilbur Puckett in our house that day holding the envelope for Mom. He looked just as sad then as he did in the newspaper photo.

Suddenly Mrs. Kean broke the silence, bursting through the screen door. She hobbled over to the tree stump, fell to her knees, and cried. I left the newspaper on the chair and sat beside her. I held her hand.

"You lost someone too. I'm so sorry," I said, resting my hand on her arm. A bee landed on her floral skirt. I swatted it away. Then Mrs. Kean did something she never had before. She squeezed my hand, looked me in the eye, and said, "Emily. I lost my Emily."

THIRTY-FIVE

Thanks to the newspaper articles—Mr. Kean's and the one in my dream—I recognized the vehicle in front of our house as an unmarked police car. I didn't want to go home and hear what they had to say. I knew everything I needed to: Dad had been murdered. The only unknown, according to the newspaper, was what would happen to his lottery winnings. But that didn't seem very important.

I completed my chores at the Keans' house, sweeping the porch and sidewalks, pulling weeds. I kept one eye on the police car. What else was there to do? Dad was dead. That thought ran through my head with each stubborn weed I yanked. Gorgeous red roses stared back at me.

Inside the house I dusted and vacuumed. I tried for the hundredth time to open the locked mystery door. Then I heard footsteps.

Mr. Kean came up behind me with the key and led me inside.

The walls of Emily's room were painted pale pink, the color of sunset in summer. Her portrait hung on the wall. I looked closer, and in the corner was a scribbled black signature: Dorothy Kean. Emily had dark hair and green eyes set a bit apart like her father's—slightly mischievous eyes as if they were concealing a secret. Her grin reminded me of Eva's, or how Eva used to smile before the accident. Chilled, I rubbed my arms.

The bed frame was painted white with pink and purple bouquets of flowers on the headboard and footboard. Mesh netting draped from the ceiling like a veil. There was a desk and a dresser and a bookcase, the top shelf lined with ribbons and trophies for gymnastics. She had many of the same books from her childhood that I did: *Charlotte's Web*, *The Giving Tree*, Dr. Seuss. I imagined Mr. Kean reading to her. I picked out one that I had never seen before, a book of German fairy tales.

"When did she die?" I asked Mr. Kean.

"Twenty years ago."

He sat in the desk chair and pointed to the bed. I sat down and he told me the story.

Emily Kean was eleven when she climbed the sycamore tree that spring day, the azaleas blooming white and purple in the front yard. Emily had climbed that tree a hundred times. Limber, athletic, and feisty, she was a gymnast who paraded around in tights, who spent hours walking on the balance beam and swinging from one uneven bar to the next, light as a feather.

But on that day, one of the sycamore's limbs, weakened by weather or insects or time, or by all three, failed her. She focused on a new bird's nest atop two intersecting branches. By the time the limb she sat on started to crack, it was too late. Emily fell through the air, grabbing at leaves and branches on the way down. If the azalea bushes had been planted closer to the tree, they might have cushioned her fall; instead, Emily Kean hit nothing but ground.

Mr. Kean had just returned home from the university. He sat on the porch with a lit pipe, rocking back and forth, marking student papers. He grinned at the paper before him. A student had titled his essay "What Is Existentialism?" and left the next ten pages blank. Amused, Mr. Kean wrote "A" in red marker at the top.

Then he heard the cracking. The yelling. The thump on the ground.

Afraid to move Emily, he placed a hand on her forehead. Her eyes rolled back. Her body jerked and twisted, then lay still.

Mrs. Kean had walked outside, color smeared on her shirt from an afternoon of painting. She carried two tall glasses of lemonade and a plate of sugar cookies shaped like flowers. It was the family's afternoon ritual.

When she saw her husband kneeling over Emily, she screamed.

The ambulance arrived quickly. Paramedics gently placed Emily on a board and raised her into the ambulance. For four days she remained unconscious at the hospital, attached to machines. The doctors shook their heads and folded their white-sleeved arms in resignation. On the evening of the fourth day, the Keans gave the order to remove Emily from life support. They held her hand as she slipped away.

Mrs. Kean stayed in Emily's bedroom for three weeks. She never picked up a paintbrush again. When that branch snapped, something inside her snapped, too. Whenever she stood up, the room spun in circles. She would hold her husband's arm to steady herself. Still, she felt as if she were always falling … falling to the floor, falling off the edge of the yard, falling out of the world she had once known.

"Dorothy doesn't want this room to change," Mr. Kean said, looking at Emily's things. "It comforts her. But I doubt it's healthy. Sometimes I think we should simply get rid of everything. But that's not healthy either."

A glint of silver on the bookshelf caught my eye–a bracelet. I picked it up and examined each of the eleven charms. The first one near the clasp was a bull. Had Emily been born in May? A Taurus? Next, a shell. Then a smiley face, a flower, the Olympic rings, a pair of ballet slippers. A life told in charms.

Mr. Kean reached for it and pressed the bracelet to his face.

"I want you to have this," he said. "Silly to have it collect dust on the shelf. It suits you."

I shook my head, but he clasped it around my wrist.

"There's nobody else I'd rather give it to."

He smiled, looking tired and serious, lost in thought. Mr. Kean, always so strong and sure, now seemed frail. Wrinkles appeared on his forehead that I'd never noticed before.

"I'll do it," I said.

"Do what?"

"I'll clean the room for you," I said. "Tomorrow. If you get a couple of boxes, I'll pack things up. You can take Mrs. Kean out for the day. Go to lunch, see a matinee. Then you can turn the room into a place that's not so sad."

I thought of Dad's clothes still hanging in the closet. Would Mom ever give those away?

"Dorothy always wanted a studio," Mr. Kean said. "She stopped painting after the accident. She blamed herself, thinking that if she had taken Emily to gymnastics practice that day … if she had been on the porch watching her in the tree … she would still be alive."

"The what-if game," I said.

Mr. Kean nodded.

"This could be her new studio." I pointed at the windows. "The light is good in here. The closet has room for supplies. She can keep her paint on the bookshelves."

"I'll talk to Dorothy about it," Mr. Kean said. He looked at Emily's portrait. "You remind me of her, Lucky. You're smart and helpful. Calmer, though."

"I wish I had met her."

"Lucky, we can't change the past. I wish I could, but it's a waste of time. Wishing for things we can't ever have."

• • • • •

By the time I walked home, the charm bracelet jingling on my wrist, the police car had left. I found it hard to stand still. It felt like spiders were crawling on my legs and I had to keep shaking them off. I paced inside the house, room to room, the same way Dad did when he memorized lines for a play. Holding a script in one hand, he'd walk back and forth, his voice rising and falling as the scene demanded.

But I had no script. When I left Mr. Kean, I had paused at the stump in the front yard and imagined Emily, a girl nearly my age, climbing that tree … and the branch breaking … and her thin gymnast's body falling through the branches and landing on the hard ground, breaking. I pictured Mr. Kean kneeling over her and how awful that must have been. Once again, I realized how quickly life could be torn from the world.

Loss. It was everywhere. Everyone has a stump in their yard, a reminder of what no longer is. I remembered smashing the dollhouse, the room and walls broken on the floor of Dad's workshop. I imagined Dad's car, crashed and burned. I saw Wilbur Puckett's photo.

How old would Emily be now, I wondered, doing the math in my head. I thought of the grandchildren the Keans would never have. I thought of the grandfather that my children would never have. Loss. Was that why Mr. Kean began reading stories to me? Was I a substitute for Emily? My heart warmed. I hoped I had brought Mr. Kean some comfort.

What had Mrs. Kean been like before the accident? I tried to picture her at PTA meetings, working at the school book fair, or baking a cake with Emily, flour dusting the young girl's pink tights. Would Mom go crazy if she lost me?

The stump looked so lonely, so sad. Dad once told me a story about a special tree that grew to heaven. I decided that I'd surprise the Keans and plant a tree beside that old stump. A tree that would grow beyond the clouds and sky. A tree that might reach their daughter.

THIRTY-SIX

The doorbell rang—or rather, the Moonlight Sonata bell tone, recently added by Danny. It couldn't be Eva, who was busy packing and shipping purchases for the eBay scholarship fund. Because the auction had been so successful, Eva now fielded fund-raising offers from other charities. It hardly seemed to bother Eva when the doctors told her that she would need another operation on her leg.

I opened my bedroom door and listened. Mom was talking to a woman whose voice I didn't recognize.

"What do you want from me? My husband is dead." Mom sounded exhausted and irritated.

"The lottery ticket," the woman said. "It was in the newspaper. I want my share of the winnings."

"Money? You want money? Why should you get any money?"

After a pause, the woman said, "I'm carrying your husband's baby."

My back against the wall, holding the door for balance, I slid to the floor.

"Tramp," Mom said, her voice even but full of anger. "You have no proof. You think you're the only woman he ever played around with?"

For a second, I thought I was listening to a soap opera on TV. But these voices were real.

"This baby is your husband's. Whether you choose to accept it or not," the woman said. "If Chase were alive, he'd have married me. I'm sure of it."

"He never would have left me. And I don't believe that's his child."

"It is. His flesh and blood." The woman's voice sounded steady and quiet. "I didn't know he was married. I don't make a habit of dating married men. I don't have to."

"How could you not? He lived here. He wore a ring."

"As charming as he was, he was an even better liar, apparently. I never saw him with a ring. He told me he was single."

I heard one of them walk across the room.

"Who's this?" the woman asked.

"That's my daughter," Mom said. "*Our* daughter. She doesn't concern you. Put her picture down."

"Well, your daughter is going to have a sister. Very soon. And I'm going to get a lawyer. That money is mine."

"Fine," Mom said. "Spend your money on a lawyer. You won't get a dime. You can line up behind the debt collectors. Our house was nearly foreclosed on. Tell you what—you can take your share of the debt."

"Take care of your own debt," she said. "I want my half of the lottery winnings."

"Well, good luck proving paternity. Did you hear? He burned in the crash. There was no DNA."

"You have a daughter. We'll do a test."

"Over my dead body," Mom said. "You're not going near my daughter."

I wanted to come to Mom's defense, but I couldn't move.

"What about his watch? The watch is proof," the woman said.

There was a pause. "Did you steal his watch?"

"He left it with me on purpose," the woman said. "He wanted me to have it."

"That watch was in my husband's family for a hundred years."

I thought about Dad swinging his shiny gold pocket watch in front of my eyes when I was little. I'd reach up, trying to grab it. The gold reflected the sun and created moving diamonds on the wall. I loved to rub my fingers over the design on the back.

"I'm not a thief," the woman said. "Chase left it at my house. I brought it here as proof. Proof that your husband was with me. Proof that the baby is his."

I got to my feet and walked like a chicken, low to the carpet, around the corner and behind the island in the kitchen. From there I saw her—a dark-haired woman, skinny but with a big belly. She dangled the watch in front of Mom's eyes as if she were trying to hypnotize her. Her bracelets clinked together. I thought of the fortune-teller in Atlantic City, the one who told me that I was lucky and then told Dad something that upset him.

The woman turned toward the kitchen as if she sensed she were being watched. Did she know I was there? I held my sliver charms to keep them from making noise. Who was this woman? She towered over Mom. Her skin was dark like the Mongellis', her black hair cascading down her back. Mom looked tiny next to her. She was younger than Mom for sure. And very pretty.

After a minute of silence, the woman turned and walked out the door.

Mom lowered her head and spoke to no one, "Good God, Chase. What else?"

I stayed hidden in the kitchen. Was this woman pregnant with Dad's baby? My sister? Mom admitted to the woman that Dad had been with other women. Why? How was that possible?

Didn't he love Mom?

Didn't he love me?

Did I really know Dad?

Loud and disturbing music filled the air. I'd never heard Mom play the piano so angrily. It matched the anger I felt.

THIRTY-SEVEN

I ran to Eva's house. The door was locked. I sat in a lawn chair, admired the calm of their porch, their summer-themed wreath decorated with sailboats, seashells, and plastic sunglasses. Four QVC packages sat piled in one corner. After twenty minutes, Silas rode up on his bike.

"Hi, Lucky," he said.

"Where is everyone?"

"The twins are at a birthday party. Dad's at a meeting. Mom's doing errands. Eva's running around somewhere. Or should I say, hobbling around. Come on in."

We sat in the living room talking and drawing. Of course, I kept replaying Mom's conversation with the pregnant woman. I thought about telling Silas.

"What's bugging you?" Silas asked. He was in the middle of drawing a storm cloud.

"Stuff with my mom. Stuff about my dad."

"I always liked your dad," Silas said. "He was fun. I had more talks with him than I do with my own father. My dad's fine, but he doesn't have the energy that your dad had."

I agreed. "He seemed revved up all the time, always having an adrenaline rush. Many people are like that. Other people seem tired, like they never get enough sleep."

"I'm not one of those tired people, am I, Lucky? I hope not."

"No. You're just right. Calm but dazzling. You used to be sort of hyper, how I picture Dad might have been in high school. Even when you couldn't talk, you still had that positive energy."

He smiled. We sat quietly, side by side, drawing. What I told Silas about Dad was true. Silas touched my face. He traced my lips with his finger. My legs tingled. He leaned in and kissed me. For a long while.

"I really like you, Lucky," Silas asked. "A lot."

I nodded. "The feeling's mutual."

"It's okay to tell me things. Even things you're afraid to tell me."

I kissed him again, then rubbed his hand. Someone was coming. We moved away from each other on the couch. We hadn't told anyone our secret. Though I wanted to confide in Eva, I was afraid it might upset her. She might think it was creepy that I was going out with her brother.

The door clicked and Eva scooted into the room. I jumped up and grabbed the bag that she held along with her crutches. Mrs. Mongelli followed behind her with other bags and boxes. Then Eva and I took cream sodas to her room.

"We shipped fifty packages," Eva said. "And we picked up more donations. This is the never-ending sale. I should pick an end date for donations, but it keeps snowballing."

I told her how proud I was about the fund-raiser.

"You sound like my father, Lucky."

Then she stopped and looked at me. She always sensed when something was wrong.

"So what's going on? You've got that funny look on your face, Lucky. The one where your bottom lip nearly disappears. What are you worried about? Is someone sick or ..."

"Dead? You can say the word. I won't melt, Eva. But wait until you hear what happened at my house."

Eva lay on her bed, her cast elevated on a pillow. "Spill it already."

"I came straight home after school. My head was killing me so I skipped my art lesson."

"At this rate you'll never finish the entry for the fair."

"That's the least of my problems."

Eva fluffed another pillow and lay back down. I thought about Emily Kean's bed, the flowers on her headboard. Mr. Kean had helped me take the bed apart. We had cleared out her dresser, too. Soon I would paint the walls a sage green, transforming the room into an art studio for Mrs. Kean.

"Tell me."

"Mom didn't realize I was home. A woman showed up and the next thing I knew, they were fighting."

"Who? The social worker?"

"No. That happened already. Good news—I get to stay with Mom."

"So who was the woman?"

"She claims that she was my dad's girlfriend."

Eva sat up sharply, knocking a pillow to the floor. "Your dad had a girlfriend? Are you serious? Did you see her? What did she look like?"

"She was tall and skinny. And young. She looked like one of those models where you can't tell how old they actually are." I pointed to Eva's stack of *Vogue*s in the corner.

"I don't get it. Why would she tell your mom that she was your dad's girlfriend?"

"Remember the article in the paper? The murderer? How he handed over the rest of his lottery winnings to the police? She says half of the money is hers."

"The lottery winnings? I'm confused. How could this woman possibly claim the money? That money goes to you and your mom. Girlfriends don't get any money."

"She's pregnant, Eva."

Her jaw dropped and she took my hand. "Why would she think it's his baby? I mean, your Dad's been dead for what—four months?"

"February 10."

"How far along is she?"

"I'm not a doctor, Eva. She's skinny, but it sure looked like she had a big basketball under her shirt."

"Why would she be entitled to the money? That's what this is all about? The nerve."

"She'll probably get a lawyer next," I said. "It's going to take a while to sort everything out anyway. The police said we wouldn't see a dime from the lottery ticket for a long time."

Eva sighed.

"Just when things were returning to normal," I continued. "Mom's working at the Stop Mart and she's starting to schedule piano lessons again. She seems more relaxed. She even planned a weekend getaway to Cape May in August, figuring we'd have a few extra dollars soon."

"Wow," Eva said. "The murder confession, the lottery ticket, and now this baby news. What did she say to the woman?"

"She lost it. The woman left and Mom started banging on the piano keys. I snuck out. She was finally getting it together. I won't be able to handle it if she starts hibernating in her room again. What if she can't go to work anymore? What if they threaten to take our house again?"

I covered my eyes, trying not to cry.

"I'm sorry, Lucky."

"My dad wasn't a liar. I can't believe he cheated on Mom. Can you?"

My stomach knotted up as I thought about what Aunt Robin had said about Eva's mother. I didn't want to discuss our cheating parents. Her mom and my dad.

"Your dad was cool," Eva said. "We don't even know for sure it's his baby. She could be a scammer. Everybody read the story in the paper. A hundred women might show up claiming the same thing."

"Maybe," I said. "Women were always friendly to him. I thought they were being nice. But a few of them, like Mrs. Hickson—the divorced lady who wore too much makeup—she was always touching him. Once I saw her feeding Dad a pastry after a show. That seemed weird."

"Well, keep your eyes open. Tell me if any other money-grubbers show up. Now would you get my laptop? Want to help me write thank-you notes to famous folks?"

I appreciated Eva's attempt to change the subject. Anything to take my mind off what happened. But no matter how many famous people we sent notes to, the face of the mysterious woman would pop into my head like a black cloud, like a bobbin floating on top of the water. I kept seeing that woman's protruding belly. Although I hoped that Eva's theory was right, a twinge in my gut told me that woman was telling the truth. And if this were so, then the father I thought I knew—well, I didn't know him at all.

· · · · · ·

I went home after dark. The air was hot and thick with humidity. Mosquitoes bit my legs and arms.

Mom wasn't playing the piano. She wasn't anywhere in sight. The evening's missed meatloaf dinner sat on the counter, cold. Then I discovered a pile of trash in the corner. Old CDs, DVDs, and videotapes stacked next to the basket. I started pulling them out. Adam Sandler stared back at me, then Steve Martin and George Carlin. The next layer contained musicals: *Phantom of the Opera, Showboat, My Fair Lady, Oklahoma, The Fantastiks*. With a paper towel I wiped off remnants of food from the cases, then grabbed a trash bag and salvaged as many as possible. Why would Mom throw them out?

I saved five Weird Al CDs. His songs still played in my head when I drew comics. I rescued the Adam Sandler CD with the famous Hanukkah song, which had been our *one* holiday tradition. Every year on the first night of Hanukkah, we lit the menorah and played the song. By the fifth night we usually forgot to light candles, but come December, that song always ran through my mind.

Then I found Dad's souvenirs. Mom must have tossed them, too. Props from *The King and I* and *Cabaret*. Steve Martin's fake through-the-head arrow and a rubber nose. The King Tut Halloween costume Dad once wore. I visualized Dad strutting through the house wearing the fake arrow, swiveling his hips, saying in an exaggerated voice, "I am a wild and crazy guy." I laughed every time. Mom had even laughed, briefly.

When I finished rummaging through the memories, my hands smelled of apple peels, potato skins, and old meat. I was full of rage. How dare Mom throw out the past. I carefully hid the bag in my closet beneath school supplies, photo albums, and clothes recently outgrown. I stared at the sack sitting on the floor like a corpse.

Then I thought about Mom. Where was she? Had she gone to work? Flaked out? After the visit from the pregnant woman, maybe she'd lost it. I understood her anger at Dad. But what was Mom capable of?

I took inventory of the house, checking every room to see what else might be missing. Something seemed wrong in the living room. It was a place I had spent thousands of hours sitting on the couch, reading comics, drawing, doing homework, watching television. What was different? It reminded me of those brain puzzles where something is missing in two similar drawings, but it's hard to figure out what. I searched the corners and the shelves. Finally, I saw a clean gray square beside a framed photo. There, the wall looked brighter, as if protected by what had hung in front of it all these years. The wedding photo—the picture of Mom and Dad's hands and their shiny new rings over the water—was gone. I thought of Band-aids, how when you pull them off real fast it doesn't hurt as much, though it leaves behind a pale mark on your skin. Why did *this* hurt so much? If things vanished from walls, could they also vanish from memory?

As I stared at the empty square, a shadow crossed the room. I turned, expecting to see Mom standing beside me. But no one was there. Only me, the empty wall, and the empty room. A trash bag of Dad's discarded life sat on the floor of my closet calling me back to the past.

THIRTY-EIGHT

I didn't sleep well. First, I heard the front door close and the lock click. Then the phone rang four times in a row. I finally drifted off. Later in the night, or past midnight, the phone rang again. Who the heck would be calling at this hour?

At five in the morning, I gave up on the idea of more sleep. I poured a bowl of Cheerios. Surprisingly, Mom was already awake and about, sweeping the kitchen floor and wiping the sink. She sat down next to me and sipped her coffee.

"What's wrong, Lucky? Why did you get up so early? Did the phone wake you?"

"Sort of. I couldn't sleep anyway."

Mom stared at the basket. "Thanks for taking the trash out. I forgot."

I had taken the garbage outside before bed—everything but the sack of Dad's things.

Were we going to talk about the pregnant woman? I sensed it in the air between us. I yawned, but Monty was certainly wide awake. He kept jumping up, begging for food. I threw him a Cheerio. He ate it and begged for more.

"Everything go okay yesterday?"

"Yup. Fine. I skipped my art lesson, though."

"Why? Where'd you go instead?"

I put my bowl in the sink, then crossed my arms. I decided there would be no more secrets. "I was here yesterday, Mom. My head hurt so I came home early."

"You were here? In the afternoon?"

"I heard her. I saw her."

Mom looked out the window into the yard. Did she want to become one of the birds and fly away? She sure looked like she did. Her eyes were puffy and red, like they'd been after Dad died.

"What did you hear, Lucky?"

Without any concealer, the scar on Mom's chin stood out more than ever before. It looked like a hook.

"She knew Dad," I said. "And she's pregnant."

Mom rubbed Monty's neck. He growled, as if sensing a threat. He'd never growled at Mom before.

"Her name is Victoria Sterling. I knew nothing about her before yesterday. But apparently she knew your father. Lucky, I don't want you to think anything bad about him. But you're going to hear things. This is a small town and people talk. I'm not quite sure what to tell you."

"What does she want from us?"

"Dad sold her a townhouse a year ago."

"So she was one of his clients?"

"More than a client."

I dropped my spoon. It clattered on the floor.

"Your father had an affair with her. At least that's what she's claiming. Oh, Lucky. You're only fifteen. I shouldn't be telling you any of this."

"I'm almost sixteen, Mom. Tell me. Please tell me."

"The baby might be his." She looked away.

"I don't believe it. Not for a second. Dad wouldn't do that to you. To us."

"She wants money," Mom said. "The lottery ticket. The money that murderer turned in. It's supposed to be ours, eventually. The police found your father's blood on that ticket. It was his ticket. The calls last night—one was from the police, one from a lottery official, another from my lawyer."

"Who else? The phone kept ringing."

"Danny. He was concerned. And hang-ups. We've been getting quite of a few of those. Probably kids."

Mom sat calmly at the table. I paced the kitchen.

"How did she know? About the money?"

"The newspaper. She read that darn story in the newspaper."

"So did I, Mom." I'd been avoiding her since yesterday afternoon. Now it had all come to light. "How much, Mom? How much is left?"

"A little over a hundred thousand."

I whistled. "And she wants it because she's saying it's Dad's baby. She's lying. Mom, was Dad a bigamist?"

"No, Lucky. He was married to me. But I am beginning to believe he was a cheater."

I noticed again that Mom's ring was absent from her finger. Had she thrown that out, too?

"Lucky, I don't know what's true and what isn't anymore. But your father had secrets. He wasn't the person we thought he was."

I recalled the sack of his music and comedy tapes, his theatrical souvenirs, his Steve Martin imitation. If I listened more closely to the show tunes and the jokes, would I be able to decipher the puzzle of the man Dad truly was? Did something hide between the lines of his personality that I'd missed? Mostly, I was scared. If these accusations about Dad were true, the bad stuff might cover up all the good stuff that I remembered until all the sweet memories slipped completely away. I had to find the truth.

"I want to meet Wilbur Puckett, the murderer," I blurted out.

"What? Lucky, you've got to be kidding."

"Don't you want to know what happened that night, Mom? In the last few minutes of Dad's life?"

"After school," Mom said. "We'll talk about it after school."

·   ·   ·   ·   ·

Instead of focusing on geometry and English all day, I thought only about Wilbur Puckett. It was going to be hard asking Mom to take me to the prison, especially since Victoria Sterling had shown up at our house. Mom had been doing so much better. I didn't want to upset her. I was afraid she would begin drinking wine again, or quit her job, or do something even more drastic. It all seemed beyond my fifteen years.

After school, Mom tried to talk me out of it. She wanted nothing to do with Wilbur Puckett. But I needed to meet him. I held firm.

"You don't understand what it's like to find out someone you loved so much was left to die," I told her.

"Lucky, I'm sorry to say I do know about that."

"You read about it, too. But I feel so helpless. I wish I could have saved him."

We were sitting on the living room couch, the site of many heart-to-heart conversations since Dad had died. Or, in our new way of thinking, *was murdered*.

"I've got a story to tell you, Lucky," she said. "A similar thing happened to me when I was a child."

She raised her hand to her chin.

"The scar? What happened, Mom? Will you finally tell me?"

"I was in an accident when I was little. No, a murderer didn't knock me off the road and leave me to die. It was worse. Someone I loved hurt me."

"Your dad? Is that why you don't talk about him? Did he die in the accident?"

"That day he died for me."

I didn't understand what she was saying. Another riddle. "Was he a bad man?"

"Not always. But when a person does something that awful, it's hard to remember anything else. It's like a big shadow blocking all the good."

Is this how I would eventually feel about Dad? Would I replace the good memories with the bad? His affairs? Impregnating a woman he wasn't even married to?

Mom paced the living room, walking over to the window and looking outside for a long while. What was she remembering? What had her father been like? With the accusations from Victoria Sterling, I wondered if I would have a similar conversation with my future daughter.

"Mom, please help me. I need to see the man who killed Dad."

"I don't want you to get hurt, Lucky. Wilbur Puckett is a murderer. Even though he's behind bars, he can still hurt you in other ways."

"But I need to talk to him. He was the last man to see Dad alive. Don't you have questions, Mom? I do."

She looked back out the window where two bluebirds landed on a branch. One flew away; the other remained perched.

"No," she said. "There's nothing I need to know."

"Well, *I* need to know. Please let me visit him. If you don't take me, I'll find another way to get there."

"I don't like the tone of your voice, Lucky."

"Stop calling me that!" I raised two fists in the air. "I'm not. I am not lucky. I haven't been lucky in a very long time."

I didn't want to cry, so I sucked in my breath. But my body began shaking and the tears refused to stay in.

"Come here," she said, opening her arms. "I'm sorry about what you've gone through. And if you honestly need to speak to this man, this Wilbur Puckett, I'll take you. But it's better to put the past behind you. I'm only trying to protect you."

I wiped the tears from my cheeks. "I want to know. I need to know."

"The answers are not always as simple as a yes or a no," she said, looking out the window. Was she thinking about the accident with her father that she still hadn't told me about?

THIRTY-NINE

Mom talked to her lawyer several times in the next few days. Wilbur Puckett agreed to meet. In fact, Mom's lawyer said he wanted to talk to me. The lawyer assured Mom that a clear partition would separate us and that a guard would be in the room. I was nervous but not scared. Wilbur Puckett couldn't hurt me. He had, after all, turned himself in.

New Jersey State Prison was located in a bad part of town, past an industrial area where abandoned factories squatted behind wire fencing. The prison bordered two towns—Rahway and Woodbridge. I had been to Woodbridge twice, both times to shop at the mall along Route One. But I had never been to this part of town. Tall fences surrounded the complex; it seemed a separate city from the rest of New Jersey. When I heard about crime on the news, I hadn't thought much about where those convicts were sent. And here they were. An American flag stood still in the muggy Saturday afternoon air.

Our taxi pulled into the visitors parking lot. I kept shivering. Mom and I both sat in the back. It cost a lot to take a taxi, but she still hadn't gotten a car, nor had she worked up the nerve to drive again. I rubbed my cold arms. No matter what I did, I couldn't warm myself up.

"It's so hot today, Lucky," Mom said. "Are you sick? We can turn around and go home. You don't have to do this."

She hoped that I'd change my mind. Staring at myself in the rearview mirror, I shook my head. I wasn't sure what I expected to discover. The night before, I couldn't sleep. My father's face appeared. The image of the Volvo crashed through my head. I saw my father bloodied and begging for his life. Now I was about to confront the man responsible for murdering him. How would I look Wilbur Puckett in the eye? What if he said terrible things that were too awful to hear?

"Can you wait for us? Or come back in an hour?" Mom asked the driver.

"I'll be back," he said. "I've got another fare in Edison. You visiting a relative?"

"No," Mom said. "A stranger. A man I've never met before."

We left the taxi and approached the gate. The building looked as if it might have been grand at one time, like the courthouses I'd seen on class trips. At the top sat a metal cap and beneath it more metal, copper that had turned green over the years. How many prisoners lived here? What did it feel like to be caged day and night? Dad once told me about a show filmed in New Jersey, a documentary called *Scared Straight!* Real prisoners and teenagers were in the movie. Its goal was to terrify young troublemakers by showing them the ugly side of prison life. Were these same hoodlums now filling the cots of this very prison?

I pulled out my Brickville High School photo ID and Mom held up her driver's license for the guard at the gate. A second guard checked a list, then put a black mark next to our names. It reminded me of the time I had after-school detention, how when I showed up Mr. Harrington placed a dark mark beside my name.

"You'll have to go in with her, Miss," one guard said. "No children allowed unsupervised."

"But I worked it out," Mom protested. "She's going in without me."

"Someone told you wrong. You have to accompany the minor inside."

Mom raised her head as if trying to find courage in the humid air. She hesitated, stopped completely, and finally followed him through the gate. More gun-carrying guards nodded to us, indicating the metal detector. We passed through, signed in, and were led to a waiting area. Was Wilbur Puckett being brought to the visiting room at the same time?

After a few minutes, a guard took us through a doorway. The room on the other side was white and plain. Bright florescent lights, one blinking on and off, lined the ceiling. Metal chairs sat in front of separate glass partitions. A phone hung on the wall next to each unit. The guard pointed and I sat down.

"I'll be right there," Mom said, indicating a chair against the wall. "Tell me when you're done."

She touched my hair and tried to smile, but her lips wouldn't budge.

My heart was beating so hard, I was certain everyone heard it. I stared through the glass at the empty chair across from me. Then a guard on the other side brought in a man I barely recognized from when he delivered a package to our house weeks ago. Wilbur Puckett, a frown on his face, sat across from me.

His scraggly hair hung long and greasy below his ears. A beard covered his face. He looked thinner than before; an apple-like protrusion jutted from his throat. A bandage patched a square of his forehead, and a fresh bruise bloomed purple as a ripe plum on one cheek. His weary eyes seemed lost.

He picked up the phone. I picked up my receiver.

"Hello again," he said, nodding.

I straightened up. "You came to my house. You delivered a package. How could you do that after killing my father?"

"It was a coincidence," he said. "An accident. I didn't know it was your house until I was there. Your dad—he wasn't wearing a wedding ring. I thought he was single. I didn't know he had children."

I leaned closer to the partition. "Why? Why did you do it? I mean, I read the paper and all, but tell me. Why?"

"My wife was dying," he said. "I was taking pills. Too many. But it doesn't really matter why. I'm sorry. I'm glad you came. I wanted to tell you most of all. I'm sorry that I took your father from you."

He looked away, then said, "I've got to go."

"No," I said, raising my voice. "You're not leaving. I need to talk to you."

He met my eyes.

"Was my father alive? Did he say anything to you before …"

"Yes, he was alive. I tried to pull him out of the car. I tried. But I couldn't. He was stuck. He said, 'Lucky.' I thought he was talking about the lottery ticket. About the winning numbers. But then I heard later that they call you Lucky. He said your name."

"My name? He said my name." I took this in, nodding. "But why him? Why did you choose him?"

"I needed the money," he said. "Your father bragged to the clerk that he had just won the lottery. I thought, at the time, that it was meant to be. My good fortune. *My* lucky day for a change. What a coincidence that I heard him saying that while I was there in the store."

"For the money. You killed my dad for the money. I read the story in the newspaper."

Wilbur Puckett told me about his wife, Winnie, who had cancer. He told me how his insurance with the local delivery service covered only a small portion of Winnie's treatment. If they had more money, Winnie would have a better chance of survival. At least, she wouldn't have to suffer so much.

Wilbur Puckett told me about his own health problems, made worse by his depression about Winnie. He took more and more medication to make it through his workdays and the long nights caring for his wife.

"I was only going to nudge your dad's car. Try to cause an accident, a fender-bender. He would have to stop. Somehow I could get that ticket from him. I wasn't thinking. I wasn't clear-headed. The meds. They made things seem different."

Wilbur Puckett stood up, still holding the prison phone.

"When Winnie died, I couldn't go on with the lie. I'm sorry. That's no excuse. You don't have to forgive me. I wanted to tell you."

Then he was gone.

I sat there, staring at the glass partition, seeing a sketchy outline of my own reflection. Suddenly I saw Dad's face, not my own.

What happened flashed before me like a dream. The blue Volvo flying off the dark road on a winter night in New Jersey, careening down a snowy ravine, the canvas sliding forward like a ghost-white passenger in the front seat. A moment before crashing into the trees, Dad calling my name. The car tumbling into an army of oak trees and evergreens blanketed with snow. The smashed windshield. The car growing hot. Dad's neck and head wet with warmth. Dad turning his face, saying to the man leaning over him, "Lucky."

The clouds in the sky. Then no light at all. Fire crackling, a muffled cry, the feather-light falling of flake after flake on the cold ground. His hand reaching out. The snow bleeding red.

What had I wanted to discover? A last great secret? He had said my name. That was something. It was what I still heard in my dreams: Dad calling my name.

What had I wanted from Wilbur Puckett? An apology? From a killer who didn't talk like a killer? He seemed sorry. He genuinely did. Even though he murdered my father, I still pitied him. He'd also lost someone.

Mom was standing next to me. "Are you okay? Ready to go?"

I didn't answer. Quickly, I walked out of the room ahead of her and the guard.

Outside, the air seemed so heavy that it was hard to move. The taxi waited.

Mom didn't say anything about my conversation with Wilbur Puckett, but she kept asking if I was okay.

"He said my name," I told her. "When he died, he said my name."

"Of course he did. He loved you. More than his acting. More than his job, more than his friends. He loved you, Lucky. Don't ever doubt that. Not for a minute."

If he loved me so much, if he loved our family, then why, why had he gone off and cheated on Mom? Why had he gotten another woman pregnant? Still, I heard his final word again.

My name echoed in the taxi. As we drove away, I looked at the flag on top of the prison. With its slight swaying, it seemed to be waving goodbye.

FORTY

When Benny Golden lost his job at the automotive plant in Edison, he began sleeping late. He started drinking vodka for lunch and dinner. The man who once played the piano and sang to young Alice Golden and her sister, Robin, stopped singing and hardly talked anymore.

I was sitting with Aunt Robin in Happy's Ice Cream parlor. With all that had happened in the past few days—a visit from pregnant Victoria Sterling and a visit to murderer Wilbur Puckett—Mom had invited Aunt Robin to stay with us for a few days. Mom thought that would take the pressure off what we'd been going through. Aunt Robin was a good listener.

But when I asked Aunt Robin to take me out for ice cream, I wanted her to do the talking. I wanted her to tell me what had happened with Mom and her father—the accident that Mom had started to tell me about but never finished. I was tired of all the secrets. I needed the truth. Now.

Aunt Robin sighed, rolled her spoon around her sundae, and told me that if I was old enough to visit a murderer in prison, then I was old enough to hear the story.

Their father, Benny Golden, was depressed about being out of work. When Mom and Aunt Robin got home from school every day, he'd be lying on the couch, asleep or watching television. Their mother would yell at him to shower, get dressed, and start looking for work.

"But our father didn't listen to her," Aunt Robin told me. "He'd stare blankly into space. He'd look at us like he didn't know who we were. And he'd fill his vodka glass again."

I couldn't imagine growing up in a house like that. Though I did recall how depressed Mom became after Dad died, how she couldn't make herself take a shower and dress for the day. She no longer took a wine bottle to her bedroom each night. But what if she had kept drinking and neglecting me? I imagined this scenario as Aunt Robin continued the story.

"I remember one time we asked Daddy to play 'Circle Game' on the piano for us. It was a song from a Joni Mitchell album that came out in 1970. He sang that song all the time, especially at night when we were little and couldn't sleep. He sang that song for years. Anyway, he just lay on the couch like a block of cheese. He would barely speak to us, let alone sing."

"What did you do?"

"Nothing. I didn't even try to interact with him," Aunt Robin said. "I hid in my room reading books, talking on the phone for hours. I was eleven. The year I started putting on all that extra weight."

"What about Mom?"

"She was Daddy's favorite. She wouldn't give up on him. They both loved playing the piano. They took walks and long drives together. One day your mom finally talked him into getting off the couch and taking her out for ice cream. I guess it runs in the family—the love of ice cream."

I smiled and slurped the remaining chocolate syrup from the bottom of my bowl.

"I remember watching them from my bedroom window. They were standing in the driveway. Daddy had lost a lot of weight since he wasn't working, but his belly still hung over his belt. I understand now that was from the drinking. He probably had cirrhosis. But your mom looked so happy that she had finally gotten him out of the house."

"What happened?"

"Daddy was trying to start the Impala. It hadn't been driven in months. Finally, he got it going. As he backed down the driveway, our mother ran out the front door, yelling at them to come back."

"Why?"

"Daddy was in no condition to drive. Your mom told me later that they were swerving between lanes, cutting off cars. She told him to stop, but he wouldn't listen to her. He kept saying, 'I thought you wanted ice cream, honey. We're going to get you a bowl of ice cream.'"

"And then?"

"He ran a red light and plowed into a busy intersection. Your mom's head hit the dashboard. A metal vent gashed her chin. She was knocked out. When she woke up, she was covered in blood. Daddy was leaning over her, telling her how sorry he was."

"So that's how she got her scar."

"She passed out again. Our mother took me with her to the emergency room. Your mom's face was bandaged and she had a concussion. She asked us where Daddy was. Our mother told her, 'Gone. Your daddy's gone.' He walked away from the crash. And he never came home again."

I thought Aunt Robin would start crying, but she held in her tears. She looked more angry than sad. She said that for years after the accident, they would automatically think it was Daddy whenever the phone rang or the doorbell buzzed. I thought about the hang-ups we kept getting at night.

"I remember one day we asked Mom how she knew Daddy hadn't died. She said, 'I wish the bastard was dead. That man nearly killed you, Alice. He was drunk and you were hurt and he left you for dead. He was only thinking of himself. He realized that he'd go to jail. What a selfish man, choosing to save himself from jail instead of saving you.'"

Now I understood why Mom had been so depressed. It was bad enough that Dad had died in the car accident. She probably was shocked to find history repeating itself. Aunt Robin must have entertained the same thoughts.

"And then that woman comes and tells your mom that she's carrying your father's baby," Aunt Robin said. "No wonder she wanted to eliminate every trace of him. Another man in her life had hurt her beyond belief."

•   •   •   •   •

Aunt Robin and I were in the living room later that afternoon when Mom answered the doorbell. A young man in a gray suit stood there.

"Alice Brilliant?" he asked, handing her a pile of papers.

"That's me," she said. "What are these?"

"You've been served legal papers. Have a good day."

She and Aunt Robin examined the documents. Victoria Sterling was trying to establish that Dad was the father of her unborn child. She wanted the DNA results from the lottery ticket as well as DNA from me.

"She's going through with this? She's really going to try to get the money?" Mom said. "Money I don't even have yet? Why? Why can't we move on?"

Mom called her lawyer in the other room, then gave us more bad news.

"He says that if the DNA is a match, it's going to be a long battle. She'll probably get part of the money. She'll have a baby that needs eighteen years of support."

"Are you kidding? That's ridiculous! What about you and Lucky?" Aunt Robin asked. "You have a daughter to support and put through college. It isn't fair. This whole thing stinks!"

Mom paced the living room, then sat down at the rented piano. She lightly touched the keys and sighed. Things had been turning around. And now this.

Aunt Robin called me into the guest room where she was packing for the trip home.

"I forgot to ask you," she said. "Any more dreams?"

"Not since the one about Wilbur Puckett being arrested," I told her.

"Well, it's time you had another. A good dream this time. A dream that will get your mom out of this mess."

Aunt Robin was right—a few days later, I had another dream. Only it wasn't a good dream. It was another nightmare.

FORTY-ONE

I woke up at seven, calling, "Mom! Mom!" No answer. I looked in the bedroom, the kitchen, the living room. Outside. No Mom, and no note on the message board in the kitchen.

Panicked, I ran to the Keans' house. Mr. Kean relaxed on the porch reading the *Wall Street Journal*.

"Have you seen my mother?" I asked, trying to remain calm.

"In fact, I have," Mr. Kean said, not looking up from the paper. "She pulled away in a taxi a little while ago. You must have been sleeping."

"A taxi? She doesn't take a taxi to work."

"Maybe she didn't feel like walking today," Mr. Kean said as I ran from his porch back home. The newspaper headline from the dream was still vivid inside my head: *Robbery at Brickville Stop Mart Kills Widow, 38*. There was no ignoring this one.

I stood frozen in the kitchen. It was Thursday. Mom didn't work on Thursdays, but perhaps she got called in. She could have taken a taxi because they needed her right away. I looked in the drawer for the address book and nervously shuffled through the pages, finally finding the Stop Mart phone number. I carried the address book to the phone in the living room, and that's where I found her note stuck under the receiver.

At the hospital. I'm okay. There to help someone else. Back as soon as possible. Love, Mom.

Who was in the hospital? Was it Danny, the boyfriend? Someone else? Why didn't she tell me more specific information? I didn't want any new secrets.

Though slightly distracted by the mystery, I spent most of the day back at the Keans' house clearing out the smaller items from Emily's old room. A few days before, Danny and I had moved out the bed and dresser. Danny hummed strange Irish ditties while we worked. Even though he couldn't carry a tune, I was glad for his help. Mrs. Kean had stopped in the doorway, held up her arms, then covered her eyes. We hesitated for a moment, expecting her to tell us to stop. Instead, she turned around and slammed the door.

Emily's room was now empty. I worked in the yard, trimming and pulling weeds. The entire time my hands were busy with tasks, I sorted through names in my head, trying to figure out who could possibly be in the hospital. Finally, I spotted Mom's taxi pulling into the driveway. I quickly said goodbye to the Keans.

"Where were you?" I asked Mom, following her into the house.

Her eyes were red and she sniffled as if she had an allergy. Or had she been crying? She definitely looked sad. What next? Had she and Danny Boy broken up? I didn't like Danny that much, but he had been good for Mom. I enjoyed watching her walk around the house with a smile and I liked listening to her singing silly love songs. Better she be that way than sad again. What if Danny left her? Would she go back to her bed, ignoring me and everyone else? Would she quit her job? Would we run out of food again? Lose the house?

"I was visiting an acquaintance. A person who's sick," Mom said vaguely.

I asked her for a name.

"You don't know her," she said.

"I know everyone you know."

"Well, we all have our secrets."

She changed the subject. I was certain she was referring to Dad and all of the secrets he had kept. The mistress. The pregnancy. The unpaid bills.

"Do you want to walk me to work, Lucky? I'm late. I need to leave now."

I couldn't believe my ears. Mom was going to work? Today? The day after my dream?

"Why are you going to work? I thought it was your day off."

"Sam called," she said. "His wife's going into labor. I have to get there as soon as possible."

No, she didn't. She couldn't go in. Not today. Not after my dream. "You can't, Mom. You can't."

"Why not? I thought you were happy I was working. I just got a raise. Sam's talking about promoting me early."

"You don't understand. I can't explain why." I pleaded with her, on the verge of begging. "Call Sam. Can't he get somebody else to work?"

"Lucky, I already told him I'd be there as soon as possible. Why don't you come with me? At least walk with me there. And bring the umbrella. It might rain later."

She grabbed her purse and headed for the door. I followed her outside, nearly running to keep up. I quickly broke a sweat. The air felt heavy with humidity, the way it gets before a summer storm.

"Mom. I had a dream. Something bad is going to happen at the Stop Mart."

"Oh, Lucky," she said over her shoulder. "Relax. A dream? Is that all?"

I had to make her understand.

"Yes, Mom. And it's not the first dream like this I've had. They have all come true."

Mom knew Aunt Robin had psychic dreams. Why wasn't she taking me more seriously? I should have told her about my other dreams before. Then she'd listen to me.

But she wouldn't break her stride. Thunder rolled in the distance.

"We should make an appointment with Dr. Brockman," she said. "We need to address these fears you're having. And those trips to the funeral home."

"There's nothing wrong with me," I said, then told her about the dreams, from the robbery to the bus crash to Wilbur Puckett.

"Lucky, your mind's playing tricks on you," she said. "Perhaps you had those dreams after the fact. Or maybe you just can't stop thinking about all the bad things in the world. I can't blame you. It's been quite a year."

There was no stopping her. We rushed through the Stop Mart doors. Sam breathed a sigh of relief when he spotted us.

"Thank goodness you're here. My wife called ten minutes ago. She's ready to go," he said, waving goodbye before Mom could respond. Two customers waited patiently as she pinned on her nametag. She rang up their purchases—cigarettes, lottery tickets, Twinkies. Meanwhile, I paced the white-and-green speckled tiles, up and down the aisles, past the candy bars, the bread, the canned goods, the paper towels, and then the whole route again.

When the last customer left, I marched up to the counter. "Mom, you can't stay here. Why can't you trust me? Aunt Robin gets these dreams. You should believe me. I have the gift, too."

She looked at me with her skeptical expression, one eyebrow raised.

"It's not like I wanted to work today," she said. "But Sam needs me. Brynn is sick. I had no choice. There's no one else to cover the shift."

"You have to leave now!" I yelled, trying unsuccessfully to keep my hands from trembling. I heard more thunder and looked out the window. It was as dark as night.

"What is it, Lucky? What do you think is going to happen?"

"You need to listen to me. We both have to leave. Now. A man is going to come in here and shoot you. A robber with a gun. I don't want you to die, Mom. I can't lose you, too."

And I burst into tears. Mom came around the counter.

"It's okay, Lucky. It's okay," she said, hugging me. "I'll call the doctor and get an appointment. You need help, sweetie."

I wanted to leave but, more powerful than my own fear of being hurt, I had to protect Mom. If I left, she would be shot. To save her and change the future, another person had to take the bullet. I decided that I might have to. Better me than Mom. Still, I had to talk her out of this, to convince her to close the store for the rest of the day. Then, hopefully, no one would get hurt.

The door jingled announcing a new customer. I turned and looked. He was a tall, skinny man with a beard and a long coat despite the heat. His dark hair was slick—it had started raining. His eyes darted from the back of the store to the register and then to us.

"Mom," I whispered. "Please."

A creepy tingling crawled up my back. I sensed the man standing near us. He smelled of cigarettes and liquor, like one of those bums I had seen in New York City.

I turned slowly, but it was too late. In the reflection of the window, a pistol flashed. The man stood there pointing a gun at Mom.

Then, at the same time, another jingle of the door. It was Silas, shaking off the rain like a shaggy dog. I tried to wave him away, but the man turned and aimed the pistol at him. Would Silas be shot too?

"Move over there, kid," the man said, waving his arms toward us. Silas obeyed.

Walking backward to the door, the man flipped the lock and turned the OPEN sign to CLOSED.

"Don't move," he said, pointing the gun at Mom, then Silas, then back at Mom again. He walked sideways behind the counter and pushed the register keys until the drawer popped open. "Where's the rest of the money?"

Mom's grip on my hand tightened. Silas slowly came up to us and grabbed my other hand.

"That's all there is," Mom said. "We just had a shift change. Most of it was deposited in the bank this morning. The rest is in the safe in the back."

The man slammed the drawer shut. He reached across the counter, yanked Mom toward him, and pressed the pistol to her forehead.

"Come with me," he said. "Get that safe open or I'll blow your head off."

He let go of her shirt, and she walked around behind the counter next to him.

"You two stay here," he said to Silas and me. "Don't move."

Then he grabbed Mom again, and they disappeared into the back room.

"He's going to kill her, Silas," I whispered, putting my head against his chest. My entire body shook.

Zap! A white flash and a terrifying crack of thunder. The lights blinked off, back on briefly, and off again. It was nearly dark in the store. In the doorway to the back, the man dropped Mom's arm, moved to the front window, and looked up at the sky. Without thinking, I took four steps toward him and, with every ounce of power, every drop of grief and anger that had been boiling in my body the past few months, I threw myself at the back of his knees. Dad had told me that the back of the legs was a person's weak spot—go low and roll, he'd said. The robber fell over. I started kicking him, pounding my feet into his side, yelling, "Leave my mom alone!"

By then, Silas had wrapped him in a headlock. That's when I saw the gun rise, point at the ceiling, and come down again. Then the gun went off.

The pain was nothing like I'd ever felt before, nothing I could have imagined. It felt hot and stabbing, radiating through my chest. Mom screamed, got down on her knees, and hugged me. I saw Silas beating the man with his fists. There was a scramble. Things got foggy. I tried to keep my eyes open, but everything turned dark. But before I passed out, I heard two sounds: another gunshot and a body thumping to the floor.

FORTY-TWO

Was I dead?

I floated in and out of a state that resembled sleep. From time to time voices sliced into fuzzy familiarity: Mom ... Silas ... Eva ... Mr. Kean. A picture of Dorothy from *The Wizard of Oz*, thrown from her house during the tornado. Dorothy on her bed, everyone leaning over her to see if she was okay. Mr. Kean's soothing, deep voice echoed in the medicine-scented room. It sounded like he was reading me a story, as he had done when I was younger, but I couldn't be sure. A siren howled. A doctor's name called over the P.A. system.

I tried to move my rubbery arm to reach the pain in my chest, but it failed to budge more than an inch. My chest throbbed. The pain reminded me of the time a woodpecker drilled a hole in the siding of our house.

Light and darkness flashed intermittently. Were my eyes open? I thought of a haunted house that Dad took me to when I was little. A room in total darkness until flickering lights gave way to skeletons, spiderwebs, and plaster heads. Was I drugged?

My mouth was dry as cotton balls. When I tried to lick my lips, my tongue stuck to them.

Time had no meaning. It might have been hours or days later when I finally opened my eyes. Mom sat by my bed.

"Where am I?" I said, realizing from the small television affixed to the stark white wall that I was in a hospital.

"St. Peter's," Mom said, rubbing my arm.

"What happened?" I only knew that the top of my chest, right below the collarbone, was throbbing.

"You were hurt, Lucky. Shot." She looked out the window as if trying to find the right words to say.

Stop Mart. The gun. The sound of the bullet. The bearded man in the long coat. It all flooded back. On the machine beside my bed, the red numbers jumped higher. My heart raced as I began to remember what had occurred.

"You saved me, Lucky," Mom said. "You're a hero. That's what the newspapers and TV stations are saying, too. You wouldn't believe how many calls I've gotten in the last four days. Reporters are standing in line to interview you."

"How am I a hero? I got shot."

"The robber was going to take me in the back room. You threw yourself at the man, knocked him down. Silas tried to get the robber's gun, but in the struggle you were shot in the chest."

I raised my hand to touch the sore spot. It was padded with bandages, a plastic tube sticking out from the middle.

"Silas? Is Silas okay?"

Mom smiled. "Silas finished him off. Boy, can he fight when he gets mad. Let's just say the robber's face got in the way of Silas's shoes. Not a pretty sight. The robber is in another hospital. Silas is doing fine."

"I remember feeling so angry."

Mom squeezed my hand. "I'm sorry that I doubted you. You tried to tell me. I don't understand how you saw that in a dream, but you obviously did. I thought you were losing it, Lucky. I should have listened. You're right. Aunt Robin is also a bit psychic. I should have known better."

"It's okay, Mom. It must have sounded nutty."

"Tell me more about the dreams."

"I don't want to talk right now," I said. My eyes felt like heavy doors shutting.

Mom raised a glass of water. I drank through a straw. It had been a long time since Mom had acted like a mother.

"I'll let you rest," she said. "I love you, honey. I'll never doubt you again."

I nodded, closed my eyes, and drifted off to sleep.

• • • •

On my seventh and final day in the hospital, after catching up with Eva, Silas, Mr. Kean, and a few other friends, and after bedside interviews with five reporters, Mom helped pack my clothes and gifts. But she wasn't herself. She paced the room nervously, grabbing flowers, cards, magazines, *Get Well* mylar balloons. Why was she so jittery? The doctors had removed the bullet and my recovery was on track. No organs had been hit. I was very fortunate.

I asked her if she was okay.

"There's something I need to tell you," she said. "I would have told you sooner but I didn't want to upset you, with all you've been through."

"I don't like secrets, Mom, so spill it. I survived a bullet. I can take whatever it is you have to tell me."

She leaned forward and smoothed my hair, which stuck up in the front. Then she told me to sit back down on the bed.

"Remember that woman, the pregnant one? You saw her at the house. Victoria Sterling, her name is. Or was."

"Was?"

"She went into labor early. There were complications. She didn't make it."

"You mean Dad's girlfriend?" I nearly fell off the bed. "She died? That's terrible."

"Yes," Mom said, "but the baby is alive. In this hospital. Downstairs in the neonatal unit. She was premature by several weeks. And she'll be coming home with us."

"What are you talking about?"

"Before she died, Victoria made a final request—that I raise her child."

"How do you know all this?"

"Do you remember where I was the morning before the robbery? Here at the hospital. Victoria had delivered the baby. But there were severe complications. Before she died, the hospital called me. I came here and spoke with her."

"This is crazy!" I shouted. "You want to raise a baby that Dad had with another woman? Why would she give the baby to you?"

"She didn't have any brothers or sisters. Her parents live in Florida. They're too old to take on a baby. I've already talked to them on the phone. They're also too sick to travel. I told them we'd visit when we go see Aunt Robin."

Mom must have read the anger on my face.

"Victoria told me she wanted the baby to have a family. And that's us," she said. "You, Lucky, are her half-sister."

I picked up my duffel bag and flung it across the room. Socks and books tumbled out. *The Fall* and *Crime and Punishment* lay like corpses on the polished linoleum.

"No way, Mom," I said. "I don't want to be reminded of Dad's lying and cheating every single day that baby is in our house."

Dizzy, I sprawled back on the bed.

"I understand, Lucky, I really do," Mom said. "I've been struggling with the same thoughts. And I'm angry, so angry at what your father did to me. To us. But then I look at this helpless baby and I pick her up, and she's so sweet. It's not her fault. Why should she have a bad life because of what other people did?"

"Join the club, sister, join the club," I mumbled, heading to the bathroom. I slammed the door and stood in front of the mirror. Angry, I wanted to vanish down the drain. Instead, I splashed cold water on my face. I didn't recognize myself in the mirror—my red, puffy eyes and oily, disheveled hair.

"Lucky," Mom said through the closed door. "We need to go. The doctor signed you out."

I had no choice, of course. We walked through the hall thanking the nurses and doctors. On the way down, the elevator stopped on the third floor. A white-and-blue *Maternity* sign stared back at us through the open doors. But they didn't need the sign to announce which floor this was. Loud crying filled the hallway. A nurse held open the door as a man wheeled a new mother into the elevator. Balloons that said *Welcome Baby Girl!* were loosely tied to the arm of the chair. The new mother glowed as she looked down at her baby wrapped in a pink blanket. A little face peeked out. I had to smile. Then the newborn's eyes popped open and she began to cry. Her mother gently rocked her back and forth, rubbing her fingers over the baby's lips.

On the way down to the first floor, I looked at Mom. She was staring at me, not the baby.

FORTY-THREE

When I opened the front door, Danny Boy stood in the hall with Aunt Robin, Mr. Kean, the Mongelli family, Baxter Geller, my teachers, and other neighbors and friends. Monty was the first one to greet me, putting his legs on my hips and whimpering for attention. A *Welcome Home* sign hung from the doorway. Helium balloons decorated the living room in a burst of rainbow colors. Framed newspaper articles announced my new status: *15-Year-Old Girl Local Hero* and *Brickville High Schooler Thwarts Wanted Criminal.*

Aunt Robin's contagious laughter filled the room. Beside her stood a man as big as a professional football player. I instantly liked him. He shook my hand and said, "I'm your aunt's sugar daddy." Then he laughed, reached into his shirt pocket, and handed me a caramel pop.

"He means the candy. He's a sugar junkie," Aunt Robin said, hugging me. She ran her hand through my hair and smiled. "Glad you're okay, sweetie. When your mom called, I was so worried. But I figured you'd be fine. You're tough like me."

"Did you visit me in the hospital?"

"I sure did. As soon as your mom called, we packed the car and Sugar Daddy drove me straight there. You were out of it, though."

Had Aunt Robin lost more weight? Her clothes seemed to hang loose and her face looked more like Mom's. But it wasn't only the weight loss that made her look different. It was happiness, I thought. She must be in love.

Mr. Kean joined our little group, hugging me tightly. Then he said something odd: "Hope you still want to work for me, Miss Moneybags." I tried to ask him what he meant, but the Mongelli twins jumped in front of me. I stepped aside to avoid being run over, and by then Mr. Kean had moved on to talk with Mr.

Mongelli, who wore his Tuesday tie. Mrs. Mongelli stood in a corner trying to talk to Mom, who held her hand in front of her face, blocking the conversation. Then she shook her head and walked away.

Eva's crutches leaned against the wall. She limped over to me without them, a great sign of progress, and held out a can of soda.

"Aren't we a sight," she said. "Limpy and Bullet Girl."

I laughed. "Hear the latest?"

"You mean besides your hero status and the reward money?"

"Reward money?"

"For catching the robber," Eva said. "He hit a bunch of stores in Jersey, New York, and Pennsylvania. The stores banded together and offered fifty thousand dollars for information that led to his arrest."

"Fifty thousand dollars! Wow. But I didn't stop him. Silas did."

Silas poked his head over Eva's shoulder. He rubbed my arm. Then he gave me a hug so hard that it hurt my wound.

"You tackled the guy and took the bullet," he said. "I was just the clean-up guy."

Winking, he took another bite of chocolate cake. I thought how strong he must be to knock a robber unconscious.

"No way. Fifty thousand dollars?" I tried to imagine how much money that was. Enough for college? Definitely enough so the pantry shelves would never be bare again. And enough until the lottery winnings came through. Danny Boy said we probably wouldn't see a dime for months.

"Yep," Eva said. "I can't believe your mother didn't say anything about it. You'll probably get the check at the ceremony next week."

"Ceremony?"

"Local hero," Silas said.

Then it was Eva's turn. "So what's your news? Can it top mine?"

"Money, sister. Money, sister," I said, moving one hand up and the other down, then vice versa, like a scale.

Eva and Silas both looked confused. "What on earth are you talking about?" Eva asked. "Do you still have painkillers running through your veins?"

"Apparently Dad did indeed have a mistress," I explained. "She died during childbirth the morning of the robbery. She left Mom the baby to raise."

Eva dropped her cup. Soda pooled on the carpet. Mrs. Mongelli appeared with a cloth. "Eva, be more careful," she said, blotting up the mess. Then she ran to the other room to stop the tornadic twins from wreaking havoc.

"No wonder your mom didn't mention the reward money," Eva said.

"Exactly."

"So you're going to have a little sister," Silas said, bumping his shoulder into Eva's. "Like I do. Now you'll understand what it's like. Good luck with that."

Eva stuck out her tongue at Silas, who smiled at both of us.

Silas kissed me on the cheek. I moved away because Eva was staring at us. "Eva, there's something we've been meaning to tell you." I looked at Silas, then squeezed his hand.

"Yeah, Sis. We're a thing. We're dating."

"I wasn't born yesterday," Eva rolled her eyes. "Puh-leeeze."

"You knew?" I asked.

"You two are so obvious. The way you look at each other. But don't get mushy in front of me. It's gross."

Danny Boy, who hovered in the background, came out of the kitchen. Instead of his work shirt and jeans, he wore a blue Oxford and tan khakis. It was the way Dad dressed when he worked at Upward Mobility, minus the green blazer. Danny still looked sloppy to me, though, like a boy playing dress-up. One shirt collar was turned halfway up and his pants were wrinkled.

"Lucky, you have a minute?" he asked, glancing at Silas and Eva.

"Sure," I said.

"I made a present for you. It's in the workshop out back. Want to take a look?"

Why had Danny gone into the workshop? As much as I was growing to like Danny, I was still protective of Dad's special place. I followed him out there. He waited a second before turning on the light. It all looked the same except for one thing—the broken dollhouse that I had left in pieces on the floor now stood upright and proud on the table. Danny had not only put it back together, but he had also finished it. The roof was complete, the exterior painted white. Roman pillars stood stately on the porch. A brass knob glistened on the front door, which had new stained-glass transoms at the top and down the side, inviting a rainbow of light into the house.

Inside, though, the house remained empty. A broken figurine lay on the side table, the one with a dark cap of painted hair. That was the father. A glue bottle sat beside it. The little man was most likely next on Danny Boy's list of projects.

What was he thinking? This was Dad's project. I wanted to yell at him, but I couldn't find the words. He just stood there, a nervous grin on his face.

"I was shot, Danny," I said. "Once you get shot, you're too old to play with dolls."

His lips turned down, dejected, like a child who had been scolded.

"You can give it away if you want, Lucky," he said. "I thought it would be nice to see it fixed up. It was a mess before. Save it for your own kids. I know you're too old to play with dolls."

"You're not my father."

"So I've been told," he said, his leg shaking and his foot tapping.

Using the tiny brass knob, I opened the front door. It was very cool-looking. Secretly, I imagined playing with it.

"Thanks," I said. "That was so nice of you."

"You're welcome," Danny Boy said. Then he left me alone in the workshop.

I wished Dad had finished the house himself. But Danny seemed like a good guy, the kind of man who finished what he started. The kind who would stick around and treat Mom well.

I walked back to the party, found Mom, and hugged her.

"Thanks for the party," I said. "I'm tired now. I'm going to rest for a while."

I decided to lie down in her room in case any of the guests came looking for me in mine. I hadn't been home for a week. Everything looked the same until I spotted two plumber's shirts hanging in the closet. On the dresser were a man's razor and shaving cream. But the thing that stood out most was in the corner of the room—a portable bassinet by the window. Inside I noticed a familiar blanket, yellow with white lambs. It felt soft. I held it to my cheek and smelled the baby powder.

I hated the idea of a bassinet and the baby who would soon arrive. So why on earth did I feel a smile spreading over my face?

FORTY-FOUR

While Mom busied herself with calls to her lawyer about adoption paperwork and lottery money, I spent my time finishing a series of comic paintings. Four days straight I spent at Mr. Geller's studio. No foster children stayed at the studio in July, and even though it seemed too quiet, I was able to concentrate on my work.

Baby Vicky, as Mom now called the rug-rat, had arrived shortly after my homecoming celebration.

"Vicky? As in Victoria?"

"Yes," Mom said. "Vicky for short. It wasn't my choice. The grandparents insisted. It was their one condition. And, of course, visits and photos."

A pained look crossed Mom's face when she told me. It must be a harsh reminder, having a baby with the same name as the other woman. I tried to ask about it, but the phone rang and Mom vanished into her room.

Our quiet house was now filled with baby cries and late-night meals, the microwave beeping its announcement of heated formula. Mom said it was an odd coincidence that I had to finish paintings for the show at the same time Baby Victoria moved in.

"You should be resting, Lucky," Mom scolded me. "You were shot. Your body needs time to heal. Forget about the art show."

"I'm fine. It doesn't hurt to lift a paintbrush," I lied. My wound still throbbed. I was tired even after a full night's sleep. But I wanted to get the paintings done. And I wanted to distract myself from the nightmares I'd been having about the robber and the shooting.

The courts had given Mom temporary custody of Vicky. Eventually they would finish the process of assigning permanent guardianship—the official adoption. Given the circumstances, Stop Mart had granted Mom a paid leave of absence. I had no idea what Mom's plans were for childcare, but no way was I going to play nanny.

I told Mom that one morning while she changed Vicky. She shook her head, then asked me if I wanted to hold the baby for a minute. I didn't.

"Come on, Lucky. I have to take a shower."

"She's got a bassinet. Put her in there," I said.

"Come on."

"Fine," I said, and reached out. She was tinier than any baby I'd ever held. While Mom showered, I touched Vicky's soft, dark hair, the same color as mine. It even curled a bit. Her skin and eyes were darker than mine, but I agreed with Mom that she resembled a little of me and a little of Dad. It took babies a few weeks to gain focus, but Vicky seemed to be staring right at me. Even smiling.

By the time Mom finished blow-drying her hair, I rested on the couch, Vicky asleep in my arms. I'd always wanted a sister or brother. The angry iceberg in my chest was finally melting. It hit me: This was my sister. But when I handed her back to Mom, sadness lodged inside me like a stone. I missed Dad all over again.

Danny Boy still came by and talked to me, but now he had a new family member to win over. He and Mom played house, walking Vicky around the neighborhood in the borrowed stroller, taking turns heating up formula and feeding her. Mom's face glowed as she watched Danny holding Vicky. She was happier than ever before. Or at least as happy as I had ever seen her with Dad.

Little by little, Danny Boy planted himself in our house, leaving tools behind or adding his own books on computers and home repair to our shelves. One day, while looking for a shirt to wear in Mom's closet, I noticed his clothes took up nearly half the space. It was stunning how quickly Mom had replaced Dad with a new man. Had Mom ever truly loved Dad? Would they have divorced if he hadn't died? Dad wasn't perfect. In fact, he was moving farther and farther away from perfection. Still, I loved him.

FORTY-FIVE

On the way to Mr. Geller's studio, I saw the mystery man again—the one in the Mets baseball cap. He walked toward me on the same side of the street. Even though his stride was long and fast, he wasn't a young man at all. I stopped to see if he would ignore me and walk past. But much to my surprise, he stopped.

Up close he looked familiar, though I was sure I had never met him. A white line slanted across his nose like a boxer's or hockey player's. It was a nose that had been broken. Below the Mets cap, his eyes reminded me of Wilbur Puckett's. They were sad eyes that had seen or done something unforgivable and had lived to regret it. Strange … his face seemed so familiar. I remembered a photo I had seen once in Mom's drawer, tucked beneath her socks.

"Are you following me, mister?" I asked, crossing my arms. Out here on the street with this old man, I wasn't scared. Nothing could happen in front of Happy's Ice Cream Parlor. But I was curious, tired of not having answers to my questions.

He looked straight at me as if trying to remember something. Or someone.

I grew impatient. It was ungodly hot, probably ninety-five degrees. Even my toes were sweating in my sandals. They made a squishing sound as I moved them against the sidewalk.

"Well? Do I know you?"

"Alice?" he asked.

"No, I'm not Alice. My mother's name is Alice."

"You look like her. Like your mother."

"I do? You know her?"

"It's your eyes," he said. "The shape of them. And that nose. That small, delicate nose. I'd recognize it anywhere."

"Everyone tells me I look like my dad. Now can you please tell me who you are?"

Instead of answering, he began humming "Circle Game," the Joni Mitchell song that Mom often sang at night when I couldn't sleep. A look of recognition appeared on his face because he asked, "You're familiar with 'Circle Game'?"

"Sure. My mom sang it to me. She always looked sad when she played it on the piano."

"Alice Golden is your mother, right?"

"That's her. And you are?"

"Please take me to her," he asked, his eyes glazing over.

"Mister, I'm not in the habit of taking strangers home."

He reached for my hand, but I pulled it away.

"Lucy," he said. "I'm your grandfather."

"Grandfather? I have no grandfathers. They're both dead. My dad's father was hit by a wrecking ball at a construction site in New York. The other—well, I'm not sure about him."

"Do I look dead?" he asked. His grin told me he might have been mischievous at one time. I didn't know what to say or do. A train rumbled by in the background.

"You like ice cream, Lucy?" The lines on his forehead and near his eyes disappeared as he smiled at me. "What do you say we have an ice cream together and talk. Then, if you want, you can take me to your mom. I've waited decades. I can wait a little bit longer."

I was shocked. "Really? You're him? My grandfather? Aunt Robin told me that you disappeared after the car accident. Was it true? Where have you been all these years?"

"Trying to forget. Trying to forget everything."

So what Aunt Robin told me was true. I didn't doubt her, but now the past—Mom's past—had come back.

"But why now? Why do you want to see Mom now?"

"A smart Jewish man once said, 'If not now, then when?' I'm old, Lucy. Soon it will be too late. I've been looking for your mom for years. When it made the news—that your dad died—I recognized the name. And here I am."

"So why are you following me? Why don't you go see her?"

"I figured she'd shut the door in my face," he said. "This way I at least get to meet you. And, hopefully, I get to see her again, too."

I was worried how Mom would react, but I had to give her a chance to reunite with her father. I followed him into Happy's and, over ice cream, we told each other our stories.

●   ●   ●   ●   ●

"Wait here," I said, leaving my grandfather in the entry hall. As I whisper-practiced what I was going to say to Mom, the word "grandfather" felt strange on my tongue. The baby stroller was gone from the hallway. Danny Boy's car was out front, so he must have taken Vicky for a walk. Mom sang in the kitchen.

A small part of me was relieved that Danny had made so many improvements to the house: the entire interior freshly painted in sunshine yellow, the driveway sealed so it looked slick and new. At first, I'd complained about the noxious scent of paint, the plaster dust irritating my eyes and throat. Now, even the ripped screen door that led out back slid seamlessly, never sticking in its track.

My grandfather looked into the music room and stared at the rented piano. Was he looking for the Steinway? He sat on the bench and inspected the new paintings on the wall. He picked up a framed photo off the piano—Mom holding me when I was a baby. He touched the glass, outlining the image with a shaky finger.

"Mom!" I called. "Are you home?"

I found her in the bedroom folding laundry—baby onesies, blankets, and a pile of Danny's work shirts.

"Lucky? I thought you were going to finish your paintings for the show."

"Change of plans," I said. "You might want to sit down."

I sat next to Mom, trying to find the courage to tell her about our guest in the living room. Then I heard the baby crying and Danny saying, "Shhh, shhh, it's okay, little one."

I ran into the hall and wedged myself between the two men as they were sizing each other up, Danny holding the baby protectively away from the stranger ... or, as I was beginning to think of him, my grandfather.

I cleared my throat. "Grandpa Golden, this is Danny. Mom's boyfriend. And this little one is Vicky, love child of my dearly departed dad. Welcome to the family."

The two men stared at each other for a long moment. Then Mom walked into the room, a stack of onesies in her hands.

FORTY-SIX

Turning away from Danny and the baby, Grandpa Golden stepped right in front of Mom. The onesies hit the floor. Mom swayed, leaned into the wall, then stepped toward him. She grabbed the bill of his Mets cap and took it off his head. She moved in even closer, studying his face as if examining a two-headed snake.

"Alice," he said.

"No. No, no, no. It can't be," Mom said. "You're dead. To me, at least."

Danny put his arm around her shoulder. "Are you okay?"

She ignored his question, waving Danny away.

"What are you doing here after all these years?" As if realizing I was still there, she looked at me. "Lucky, did you let this man into our house?"

I nodded, realizing I'd made a mistake. How could Mom forgive him after all these years? Then I had another thought: If Dad suddenly appeared, could I forgive him?

Grandpa Golden put out both hands, pleading his case. "I'd been searching for you, Alice. When I read the article in the paper about your husband's death... I'm sorry for so many things. Can I talk with you? I have so much I want to say."

"What's the point? Why don't you go back to playing dead? You crash your car and leave me to die on the road, and now you want—what? Forgiveness? To meet your grandchild? Too late. Sometimes it's just too late." She shook her head back and forth. "For years I waited for you to come home. Years. And you choose now? No."

She side-stepped past him and opened the front door for him to leave.

"I don't expect your forgiveness," he said. "I only wanted to see you, to see that you and your family are okay. That's all."

I didn't want it to end here.

"Mom, give him another chance," I said, blocking Grandpa Golden's way to the door. "Please. For me. I get why you're mad. But I sure would like a grandfather. I've never had one. Look, you gave me a sister. Why not a grandfather?"

Mom turned to the street. It seemed like she was looking at the Keans' front yard. Her shoulders started shaking. She put her hand over her face and shut the door. Then she led Grandpa Golden to the kitchen.

I stayed in the living room with Danny. I was struck by Danny's pink Polo golf shirt. The bright color looked good on him. I smiled. He wasn't Hollywood handsome like Dad, but he wasn't bad for an old person. His expression had a child-like softness. I understood what Mom liked about Danny. He was easy to have around. He didn't talk too much and he didn't demand center stage.

"Lucky," Danny said, "how'd he end up here? Did he just knock on the door?"

"No. It sounds ridiculous, but I thought my dad might be alive these past few months. Well, not alive, but that he was following me—or that his ghost was. Turns out Grandpa Golden's been the one following me. He's been trying to work up the guts to see Mom again."

"That makes sense," Danny said. "To me at least. When my grandfather died, I thought his spirit was hanging around. I even had dreams where he gave me messages. Our minds do weird things when we miss someone."

"Oh, I get it. Mom told you about my dreams."

"Yup. But now she believes them. Believes you. That you have a kind of special intuition about the future."

"I don't know what to think anymore," I said. "For a while I didn't believe Dad was dead. There was no body. I thought someone else had died in the wreck."

Danny glanced at Vicky, who slept in her bassinet. "It's hard to fathom that a person you love can die. Your mind doesn't want to."

He smiled at me and nodded toward the kitchen. We couldn't hear voices anymore, so we got up and peeked in to make sure everything was okay. Mom and Grandpa were sitting quietly at the table drinking hot chocolate on the hottest day of the summer.

"Join us," Mom said, waving us in.

And so we did.

Endow the living with the tears you squander on the dead.

—Emily Dickinson

FORTY-SEVEN

ONE YEAR LATER

On a rainy Monday in late August, a policeman arrived at our doorstep and rang the bell. Danny had left for work. Vicky slept in her crib. I sat at the table working on a new set of drawings.

Mom scrunched her nose, recognizing the policeman. Was it one of the officers who had shown up with the news that changed her life—our lives—on that February day that seemed like a lifetime ago?

"Mrs. Brilliant, may I come in? I have something for you," he said, shifting a small box to his other hand.

Mom opened the door wide and led the officer into the living room. He stopped short and squared his shoulders.

"We found your husband's remains. We're sorry for the delay. They were misplaced. We found this, too," he said. He raised a clear plastic bag. A glint of light reflected in Mom's eyes. He pulled it back for a second as if not wanting to give it to her.

"Sign here," he said, handing her a piece of paper attached to a clipboard.

After Mom showed him out, she sat in Dad's chair and pulled a ring out of the plastic bag. The diamond glittered in the overhead light.

"Mom," I said. "What is it?"

"An engagement ring," she said. "The ring Dad bought for Victoria Sterling."

So this was the answer to our final question—Dad had planned to marry Victoria. He was going to leave Mom for another woman. My heart sank. Wasn't a ring a promise? Were all promises made to be broken? Mom seemed a little sad, but she put it back in the bag and forced a smile.

Mom wore her new ring. Danny Boy had proposed before he officially moved in, though he'd been living with us, more or less, for much longer. Mom gushed when she talked of wedding plans. She wanted me to be the maid of honor. I was happy for her, but I still felt gloomy when I recalled the old wedding photos of Mom and Dad that once hung on the walls.

One thing I didn't miss were the nightmares. They died when the bullet entered my body. Now my dreams were full of trees and flowers. Aunt Robin told me that her prophetic dreams come and go. I hoped that wouldn't be true for me.

I walked outside with Monty and looked across the street at the Keans' new memorial garden. It had replaced the stump of the tree that had ended Emily's life. Sometimes I watered the flowers or pulled weeds there.

Silas appeared and we sat on the front steps. Monty licked his hand. I touched the heart locket he'd given me for my sixteenth birthday. I carried a small photo of him inside. On my bracelet from Mr. Kean, I now wore a lightning charm that Silas had given me when I left the hospital.

"Ready for school next week?" Silas asked.

"Ready as I'll ever be. Senior year. I can't believe it."

Silas was a freshman at the local college, but he promised to drive me to school every day. Eva would ride with her boyfriend. We were still best friends, but she gave me my time with Silas.

While Silas and I were sitting on the steps talking, a deer wandered around the side of the Keans' house and walked toward the garden. It was a fawn. Her glossy eyes stared back at me. I wondered where her parents were.

I missed Dad.

The front door opened and Mom came outside with Vicky. My sister's face lit up when she saw me. "Lucky!" she yelled, then toddled over and climbed into my lap.

ABOUT THE AUTHOR

Maureen Sherbondy is an award-winning writer whose short stories have appeared in *The Stone Canoe, The North Carolina Literary Review, The Cortland Review,* and other journals. *The Slow Vanishing* is her short story collection. She has also published nine poetry books. Maureen lives in Durham, North Carolina, with her writer husband and her cat Lola.

NOTE FROM THE AUTHOR

Word-of-mouth is crucial for any author to succeed. If you enjoyed *Lucky Brilliant*, please leave a review online—anywhere you are able. Even if it's just a sentence or two. It would make all the difference and would be very much appreciated.

Thanks!
Maureen

Thank you so much for reading one of our
Young Adult Fiction novels.
.If you enjoyed our book, please check out our recommendation
for your next great read!

What the Valley Knows by Heather Christie

"A taut, compelling family tale."
-Kirkus Reviews

National Indie Excellence Awards- Young Adult Winner
Readers' Favorite Gold Medal Young Adult - Coming of Age
Maxy Awards Young Adult Winner

View other Black Rose Writing titles at
www.blackrosewriting.com/books and use promo code
PRINT to receive a **20% discount** when purchasing.

* 9 7 8 1 6 8 4 3 3 5 4 5 9 *